DEDICATION

For Martin, as always.

LONG BEACH

AND

OTHER SHORT STORIES

HELEN VAN ROOIJEN

ACKNOWLEDGEMENTS
Long Beach - and Other Short Stories

Again, this book of Short Stories has taken me a long time to write and compile.

I started writing and telling short stories, very young. My father would tell me a story about a 'Rascal Rabbit'. Some were made up on the spot because I demanded them each night, and after his telling, I would reciprocate with my own story. Poor Dad, I suspect mine were a skewwhiff plus version of his; but it was my start.

Later at school, more than once my teachers told me – in confidence – that they often put my essays and examination pieces to read last – because my History, English or other, even Science efforts, were always interesting. These may not have had any dates in the history and the facts would usually come from other readings, but I wasn't just rehashing the lessons. My imagination, and ideas, were from other sources, rather than books I was supposed to be reading. I passed the exams anyway.

Later, I tried the same with ambulance and social work degree examinations but that didn't go down quite so well with those tutors! But again, I passed.

However, over the years I have submitted stories to competitions and won many awards. My first computer came from one such competition, and I loved it. Sadly, it is now way out of date and this latest one delights in correcting, or giving me suggestions, with my slightly dyslexic spelling etc.

Enough of that! I love writing stories about people, places, my family history, plus a little science fiction creeps in, as well. My greatest love is writing mystery and crime novels, but poetry and short stories remain part of my repertoire.

As usual, I thank my husband, **Martin van Rooijen**, who has done most of my covers, with probably too many suggestions and requests from me: and to **Mary Gudzenovs**, a magician at putting my books together for printing. Thanks to **Diane Hester** for the gum tree photo on the back cover. I couldn't do without you all.

OTHER BOOKS BY THIS AUTHOR:

Novels: Rendezvous at Lock 6

                    Rendezvous on the Opal Fields

                    Rendezvous with Death

                    The Silence of the River

Coming soon: The Silence of the Manor

Poetry: Life is Not a Stranger

CONTENTS

LONG BEACH

The long beach curved pale and dimpled in the morning light. 'Rather like these last days,' Tom thought.

He cast his fishing line toward the blue weed line and watched the red float bobbing in the ripples. It didn't matter if he caught none of the tommies or garfish slipping silver through the water, just being there was all that mattered.

His last summer.

Today like yesterday, and all the weekdays, the small figure appeared on the beach, far off.

The girl was six or seven years old, he reckoned. She always wore a long-sleeved shirt, bathers, she was bare footed, and carried a cotton shoulder bag. A tumble of brown sun-bleached curls hung against her pale cheeks and down her back. Choosing a shell here a pebble there, she picked her way towards him, then squatted five metres away. She lay her treasures out in patterns inside a ring of sand before her and watched him seriously from behind her fringes.

Tom glanced behind him to Laura, his wife of thirty-four years and many life voyages. As usual she had her yellow sketchpad and pencils in hand and sat relaxed on the tartan beach blanket. They exchanged a smile at the delicious sameness of these special days.

For three weeks the early morning fishing forays had brought this other catch – the small child, silent and always alone. Today, she finished her patterns and came to stand closer, ignoring Tom's eyes and smile.

He reeled in another tommy-ruff and plopped it into the tin bucket. The fish swam in panic circles with the other sprats. At this splashing commotion in the water the child came nearer and peered into the bucket.

'Can I have a fish?' she asked. 'Please.'

'Of course you can,' he said in surprise. This was the first time she had spoken to them on these morning rendezvous. 'Have you got something to put it in?'

She pointed to the fish she wanted and held out sandy hands. Bending to catch the small fish wasn't easy, the effort making Tom wheeze and gasp. The child stared into his face and then clasping the wriggling fish to her shirtfront she backed away. In a few steps she was ankle deep in the sea and had released the fish. It sped away. She splashed foam after it and turned back to the beach. Her smile and giggle embraced him.

'Thanks,' she called and was gone in flying leaps and skips.

The effort and excitement had tired Tom and he packed away his fishing gear. He joined Laura, kicked off his shoes and luxuriated in the dry sand under his feet. Laura reached to touch his arm, the contact reassuring her. They rested, shared their thermos tea and watched a lone dolphin hissing troughs in the blue silky waters. Laura showed him her sketches. She had the talent of making a few pencil lines easily depict a scene and today she had drawn the moment of the fish's release. He chortled at her capture of his stocky figure in a surprised posture and the child's fluid throwing action halted on paper.

They spoke gently of this child and these summer days almost gone; of their children grown and compared past summers of family beach activities. There were no grandchildren yet as their children and their partners were immersed in careers, study, and setting themselves up. The family wanted Tom to remain in medical treatment and had argued strongly against this delaying holiday. Tom and Laura had seen the anguish, the resignation and love in their eyes. The unknown child they saw each morning represented grandchildren unborn and future times unshared and unsharable. They accepted this and took the mornings as gems they could not explain for themselves.

Before they left the beach, they stood beside the patterns the child had made that day with her gatherings. It was usually a circle or little waves but today she had made a swimming fish. A fish inside a circle of sand and stones.

Next morning the child arrived as usual.

Her picture of a man holding a fishing rod made, she wandered over to stand beside Tom. The sea washed gently in before them and the backwash shell and grit hummed and sighed. When Tom nodded to her, she chose a garfish and set it free. The child tasted the fish's salt on her hands, wiped them down her shirt, and giggled. She paused long enough in her departure to glimpse Laura's new drawing.

On weekends they went to the beach as usual but the mornings lacked the fascination of the weekdays. They thought they saw her in the distance with a woman but the sands remained empty near them. They didn't really want to know more of their mystery child as they referred to her, the wonderment of her being there each weekday was enough. Additional involvement would probably be too much to cope with now.

Monday morning was almost longed for, and they were waiting in their positions on the long curve of the beach when she appeared.

Tom had caught nothing: no fish for tea tonight.

The child sat quietly nearby playing with her shells, making and remaking her patterns. Soon she wandered close enough to see the sketch on Laura's pad but shyly refused the offered biscuit. Finally, Tom caught a fish and hopping from foot to foot, she waited as he unhooked it.

It was hers, released and again she ran off.

Laura caught her breath. The pattern today showed the fish escaping from the confinement of the stone circle. She knew the age–old sign – death – and buried her face against Tom's shoulder.

Thursday was their last day at the beach. The summer was almost over and with it their tenancy of the beach house. Now it was time to go back to the city, to be within the warmth of their waiting family, and to face the continued treatments. That evening as the sun set and twilight settled as a comforting haze across the sea Laura framed a sketch of Tom and the girl on the beach. She planned to give it to the child. Tom checked his fishing box and retied hooks and traces for the last time.

In the morning Tom caught a brimming bucketful of fish. The girl came slowly toward them swirling sand in circles with her toes. She put the pebbles and shells in a heart shape on the corner of their blanket and received the sketch and a hug from Laura. Slipping the gift into her shoulder-bag she ran down the beach slope to Tom.

The ceremony of releasing a single fish was concluded and she stood there still. Tom gave her another fish and another. She danced around him shouting and laughing as together they flung the slippery sprats into the waves. Again, and again the fish flashed free and finally the bucket was empty.

'Thanks,' she called, her laugh lilting over the waves soft murmuring. Tom bent to her and she touched his face. Then she ran back along the sands and was gone.

Next day the long beach stretched empty.

FOXES

'Match speed,' the Pilot said quietly.

The helmsman eased the yellow Pilot boat into the lee of the huge freighter. The morning was fair with seas blue and dappled. Dolphins had accompanied the Pilot boat out to sea and still played under the bow.

'OK,' the Pilot continued, 'usual drill.'

He nodded to the two regular members of the crew, then caught hold of the rope ladder and swung up and aboard to the ship's deck high above. With the freighter Captain's permission, the Pilot took control on the bridge to guide the way through the maze of islands that guarded the mouth of the port estuary. The stubby harbour tugs slipped into station alongside and began the manoeuvres that would bring the freighter safely into harbour.

The third member of the Pilot boat crew, ignored on instruction, watched and waited as the ship was brought closer to the wharf. In his attempts to look a part of the working crew, he almost missed the brief shard of light from the second porthole on the starboard side of the crew's quarters.

'Yes! Got you!' the third member triumphed to himself.

The wharfies berthed the ship, hauling taut steel hawsers that bound the ship in the uneasy alliance of any ship to the land. Last orders were called from the bridge; the Pilot exchanged final pleasantries with the captain, and came off as the Customs men clattered up the gangway for their usual ship's inspection. The ship and its crew settled into shore duties.

There were a few tourists and fishermen on the wharf observing the ship docking. Nothing out of the ordinary, so far.

Nothing to indicate that an illegal drug shipment was on board. One that would be smuggled ashore in the brief time it took to top up the grain load before the ship sailed again that evening.

Just that mirror flash of light.

Finally, the customs men left. They'd found nothing, as expected. The ship slumped lower into the water as grain swept along the conveyer belts and down into the caverns of the hull. A few empty-handed crewmen went shore apparently intent on shopping in the harbour town. They reboarded an hour later loaded down with supermarket bags and boxes of small electrical goods.

Nothing suspicious. Nothing unusual. Nothing yet.

The day's weather stayed clear and mild and the third crew member waited. Waited and watched. This was better than office duties or clambering up and down gangways into the dark, oil smelling, steel innards of the ship's holds. He stripped to the waist and enjoyed himself as he polished the brass lanterns, woodwork and pretended deck maintenance jobs. He was undercover and his surveillance vigil was set up after a telephone tip-off.

'Stay on deck. You've got to see something,' his Custom's CO had advised that morning over breakfast.

The ship sailed on the high tide as the sun set. Everything went smoothly, the ship was ushered out of the harbour and the Pilot boat returned to her berth. Her normal crew departed and the Custom's CO came on board with two other officers. The third crewman prepared to go ashore.

'Nothing to report,' he shrugged to his CO. 'Boring as hell! Got a bit of a tan though.' He stretched expansively, his face amused as he reached for his backpack of spare clothing and lunch box.

The Customs chief moved forward and slipped the pack out of his reach. A sheaf of photos, taken that day by a pseudo tourist, was fanned out on the chart table. In two photographs the customs officer was not evident on the Pilot boat's deck.

'Why aren't you in these photos?' the CO asked, eyes cold and grey hard.

'You were ordered to remain on deck.'

'Call of nature,' the officer grinned, shrugged at the other officers and attempted to laugh his absence off as trivial. The faces around him remained impassive. Giving nothing away.

'And what about this photo?' the CO demanded and threw down the last print. The officer was just visible sheltered by the boat's wheelhouse. He was dragging on a line, pulling something out of the water.

Now his smile and high colour faded.

The CO's hand reached into the officer's pack and withdrew a bulky square plastic wrapped parcel. A parcel of drugs.

'Yeah, right,' she said. She spoke to her second in command. 'Arrest him!' Get him out of my sight.' She turned away in disgust.

There was a brief struggle and cursing as the arrest was made.

The CO pulled her long hair free of her confining uniform cap as she turned back to the offender. Her eyes reflected a sadness, but her voice was a grim offering, no compromise to her former lover.

'You won't be home for dinner tonight.' She paused. 'Tonight... or ever.'

WALKING WITH GRANDDAD

'Lift your face,' his gentle voice instructed. 'Smell the wind.'

'Why?' I wailed.

The voice insisted. 'It's all right. Do it.'

My sandals kicked the leaf litter into irritable mounds. We were lost and he wanted me to smell the wind!

The path had petered out and the mallee scrub stood a tangled green-grey barrier I could smell wattles. Eucalyptus.

'What do you want me to smell?' I said.

'Do as I ask,' he repeated.

'But we're lost...'

When I was a child my family and friends went for picnics in the Port Lincoln National Park. On arrival the children would scramble to get the picnic baskets unloaded and firewood gathered for our barbecue. We'd run wild for the first hour and flop onto spread blankets for lemonade before starting the next adventure.

That's when Grandad would pounce.

Just before lunch.

'Let's go for a walk,' he'd say.

My reluctant seven-year-old elbow would be caught firmly. His walking stick in hand, his hat on his head, a pipe clenched between smiling lips, and he was ready for our walk along the meandering tracks. I wanted to be off catching tadpoles with the other children but the old Scot would have none of it.

He knew every bird song. He'd hear them, despite denied old age deafness, before the call had registered in my ears.

'Have you spotted the bird yet?' He'd ask and his walking stick would point. 'It's up there "Sure enough there'd be a bird high in a tree. Sometimes there'd be a flash of parrot feathers – emerald, red and gold. 'Listen!' He'd say with excitement in his voice, 'The birds have gone quiet. Can you see a hawk anywhere?'

We'd find orchids in the underbrush, some so small I'd have trodden on them without his instruction. I'd smell lemon scented gum leaves crumpled between his fingers and in return I'd thrust native flowers under his nose.

'This's pretty.'

Pretty is not a description,' he'd grunt in exasperation. 'Describe things properly. Tell me what you see.'

I'd try and he'd encourage the words from me.

But today we were lost.

I sniffed. Maybe I could smell something.

'Smoke?' I hesitated.

'What type of smoke? Come on Lassie, be specific.'

I sniffed again. 'I can smell the sausages cooking for lunch!' I said in triumphant.

'Good,' he answered. 'Now. What can you hear?'

I listened.

The trees shuffled branches around us.

'Only bush noises,' I said petulance creeping back. But there was something else. A click.

'They're playing cricket. Someone's hit the ball.'

'Where? What direction?' he demanded.

I lifted my face to the wind and turned until my ears were sure. 'Over there!' I said grabbing his hand.

'Take me back.' He smiled. 'It's lunch time.'

After that I demanded our walks. Granddad's magic had taken hold. He died when I was twelve, so I had half a dozen good years of walking with a legally blind man and learning to see.

CONCORDE'S LAST FLIGHT

The two old men sat within metres of each other on the stands erected at the Heathrow Airport perimeter fence.

Both waited.

One sat with a boy at his side. A young boy, of about seven years of age, who talked excitedly non-stop. Over the hours as they waited the old man, as a grandfather would, fed him sandwiches. Later an ice-cream from nearby shop and answered the boy's questions. Not that there was need to answer many questions. The boy knew his Concorde.

The other old man sat alone and watched everything. Watched without appearing to watch.

Both men knew the Concorde's story.

Both knew the history of when the undercarriage of the French Concorde had flared for a milli-second before a fireball of flames leapt out of the port engines. The witnesses, on that day at Charles de Gaulle airport, reacted in horror as the aircraft took the accidental fiery plunge to the ground. One of the old men, coincidentally there that day, impassively regarded the scene while his face registered a similar expression to those people around him.

Disbelief. Shock. Horror.

He was a good actor.

He filed that image. That moment in his memory and his plans started then. In another time and another place, it could become his masterpiece. His final stage play.

His own escape.

For 60 years he had been adept at disappearing when the

world agencies got too close. This next stop would be his final retirement in South America where his enemies could not follow, even if they suspected he was still alive. A country without extradition laws would protect him. For a price in American dollars. He had the dollars and he was used to paying for his safety.

The old man knew Concorde well. He had often paid the ridiculously high prices to fly in the Englander's pride. His lip curled, 'Flag carrier of the airline.' The uncomfortable but fast aircraft was the rich industrialist's symbol of success. The famous flew in her but it was the rich that had kept her in the skies. Until the French accident started the downward financial spiral.

To today.

Concorde's last flight was today and he had a seat. He smiled. He had not even paid for it but was granted the seat as an honoured frequent flier. Such an honour!

The plans were complex. He had found an unremarkable misfit on the New York streets. An older man who resembled him. That's all he had to be. A doppel-ganger. Making the facade complete with clothing, make-up, his own passport and training. How to be a very rich man. A statesman. He had fed a ruse story to the vagrant with ample money. Promises of more. Plenty more – afterwards.

Afterwards.

That was a laugh!

There had been no problems. Easy really for a man of his experience to devise cover stories and master plans.

The imposter was now sitting in his seat on Concorde. Maybe he had looked at the curvature of the Earth encapsulated within the fragile layer of atmosphere. Grey Atlantic seas heaving and rolling kilometres beneath the wings and dark space above. Maybe he was drinking champagne, eating lobster salad, smiling and flirting with the attendants.

Soon it would be over.

His unlamented third wife, who awaited his arrival in Paris

ready to join a cruise ship, would travel on alone. Apparently, a widow. So be it. She was no loss. He smiled. He was probably no great loss to her either. They were a trophy couple. She young and beautiful: he much older and rich. Very rich. As happens with wives, getting her to go ahead to London and Paris from New York without him had proved only a minor hiccough. Remedied with an open credit card. It always worked with his wives.

He had to be present at the airport for his final masterpiece. He could have planned it to happen over the Atlantic but where would have been the drama in that? None for him. He had to conduct his ultimate master-class.

Waiting was always the hardest.

Always waiting to see the results of his handiwork. An honoured guest at assassinations. Seen but not seen in the crucial moments. Not always as himself, but always there. The factor in the incident that no one remembered. A phantom. No one out of place on films or video. The perfect paid killer. The killer of kings... and presidents.

Hence this cold evening he was one of the crowd. Someone who had paid for his seat in the grandstand. Waiting with the other Concorde fans. Smiling. Keeping up the pretence. Pretending that he had never flown in Concorde.

'Could never have afforded it,' he smilingly told the people waiting with him on the hard seats. Been proud that Concorde was British. Ready, with them, to shed a tear at this final history making flight. O yes!

Concorde had taken off from New York, amid Yankee fanfare, almost three hours ago.

It would never land safely.

Obtaining and planting the miniature incendiary device? This was not a problem for him within his world of terrorists, crime bosses and little wars. Munitions were always available to those with the money. The money and the knowledge. Munitions made by all nations. Left over munitions from fallen regimes. Bombs sold clandestinely on the world black markets for huge profits. He had traded himself at times.

Suddenly there was a crowd intake of breath.

A shudder of anticipation.

The first of the three Concordes was in sight. The one from Edinburgh. Another from Spain followed in celebration attendance. To add to the spectacle of the last passenger flight from America.

British Airways Flight 002 from New York would land last.

The white swept back moth-wing shapes were momentarily visible between the autumn clouds above London.

Flight 002 flew in formation behind its heralds.

'There it is!' the boy shouted to the fat woman beside him. He waved his Union Jack madly in the direction of the ultimate speck that flashed now as the plane turned and lined up the airport marker lights.

The fat woman shouted. Her voice was drowned by the shriek of the first Concorde landing. The second followed in a wallop of sound. Of thundering reversed engines. They begin the slow taxi around Heathrow. Flags flapped proudly out of cockpit windows and fire engines flooded the air with water jets. Water could be used more productively in a little while. For the fires. For the wreckage. His thoughts were wry but his disguised face beamed. For the fat lady. The boy. For the TV cameras.

His time was coming.

Listed among the dead, his release was coming.

Flight 002 from New York swept in. The beautiful shape lined up at the end of the runway.

Bomb mechanism was set to explode at precisely 10 metres of altitude. 10 metres from safety.

The wheels were down, in landing position, and the sleekest bird had its talons out to grab the earth. It appeared to hover reluctant to commit itself to the earth. Poised.

Waiting for contact.

The pilot would want to make the perfect landing. He would have done it hundreds of times but today would be his last. The nose cone was drooped. The rear wheels ready; touch, hold it down, no little bumps, then ease down the nose wheel. He would have rehearsed it in his mind. The consummate professional performing for the world.

The perfect killer understood the perfect pilot. He would never get the chance to show off the last immaculate landing.

British Airlines Flight 002 from New York landed safely.

Perfectly.

The crowd roared. Screamed its delight at perfection.

The old man stared. Gasped! He had failed!

As heavy hands grasped his shoulders he felt the first shooting of pain across his chest. As though the Concorde had landed on him. The weight was unbearable. He crumpled under the seats and between concrete and sky he looked into knowing eyes. The other old man's eyes. Young eyes in an old face. His own doppel-ganger from New York was arresting him.

He was set up! A sting. The ultimate sting!

He cursed himself. He should have known...

The fat woman shrilled her laughter as she pulled off a shabby grey wig and unbuttoned the padded coat. Through professional ageing makeup his wife's steel eyes locked onto his.

Another curse foamed off his lips...

Then a black screaming spinning void.

The still innocent boy from the orphanage's glowing eyes followed the slender aircraft as it slowed to a stop at the end of the runway. Rented for a day, like the doppel-ganger, he'd had his thrill of Concorde.

Before the Concorde had turned to taxi back towards the terminal and the waiting celebrations, the old man was gone.

Lifted as garbage. Whisked away as all eyes watched the grounded sleek white bird begin the parade around the airport to receive its final homage.

Retired.

Both retired.

JIM AND MR PETER

On the third morning of the early spring storm old Jim's body was found on the beach. When, the day before, Mr. Peter's corpse and the splintered woods of their clinker-built dinghy were thrown up by the sea, the police and the shack people knew old Jim must be gone too. His neighbours sat with Jim quietly waiting until the police had looked, probed, and taken their photos, and the coroner's van came to take him away for the necessary government final reckoning of his life. Then they would get him back to bury him, with his friend, in the little bush cemetery near the shack town.

People knew Jim well, for it seemed like forever since he and his old mother had arrived and had settled into the coastal-dune holiday shack community. She cared possessively for her simple natured, man-child son and most people had forgotten her name if it were ever first given. One day however, she was taken off to hospital after a 'wee turn', and died within the week. Jim just stayed on looking after himself in his tiny hut, overflowing with beach-combing treasures.

The years rolled on. Jim, clad in an odd assortment of found clothing and woollen hats, played with the children on the summer beach. He taught many to fish with hand lines and to whittle driftwood. Twisting up his face, Jim would make the bird calls, seeming to communicate with his feathered friends with ease. He was trusted as the friend of the children over the years and he never betrayed that trust.

When the community built wooden swings for the children, Jim put seaweed and sand under them to soften the ground against the children's falls. 'Come on', he'd shout to the children, 'You can swing now. It's safe now.' And they did. Taking his laughing turn on the swings he was pushed by the children and walked all wobbly when he got off.

Jim patrolled the line of shacks after storms tidying debris, and, delighted by the shape of beach stones, he collected thousands and edged the pathways between the shacks with them. He was given a pot of white paint and the shack area took on an ordered and festive look after he painted the stones. He fished from his little boat on calm days and shared the fish he caught. People brought an extra loaf of fresh bread, some fruit or a chocolate bar for him when they went to town shopping.

Then Mr. Peter arrived. He appeared one day at Jim's side and was proudly introduced as his friend. The shabby, bewhiskered pair were always together, sharing everything and Mr. Peter sat in the bow of the little boat when old Jim fished. They ate a simple diet of fish, bread and tomatoes, potatoes and cabbages from their garden. It was all they needed, but when there was a summer barbecue anywhere along the line of shacks they were expected. 'Come on Mr. Peter. We are going to have sausages', old Jim would call, and they would attend. They both loved ice cream and smacked their lips savouring the taste.

One autumn evening Mr. Peter appeared, very distressed, at a neighbour's shack. They went home with him to find old Jim had fallen breaking his hip. He was taken to hospital where it was discovered Jim had no income and no Medicare number. He didn't exist in records and he was not even sure of the spelling of his name. The hospital social workers, after righting these wrongs, were concerned about him coping when he got home – and so the problems started.

The officials were shocked to find there was no electricity connected to the shack; candles for light, and cooking over open fires – 'so dangerous considering.' As they were not told that the old friends often slept in their 'outside lounge', on worn chairs and an old settee, with the sky, sheoaks and gum trees as their ceiling, their sensibilities thus were not further outraged. However the well-meaning bureaucracy had the opinion that 'something had to be done.'

Old Jim recovered, and with Mr. Peter, continued on seemingly immune to the halo of perceived problems around them. They limped their gray-haired way around the shack area, with Jim using a splendid dolphin handled walking stick he had carved himself. Mr. Peter's legs were somewhat shaky but they covered the distances they had always walked. The garden beds were dug ready for planting tomato seeds on the first warm spring days, when the government cars returned.

The words were kind, reasonable by any standards, and final. Jim and Mr. Peter could not stay safely where they were and must move immediately to a 'lovely little unit' in the town. Old Jim listened and both nodded with apparent comprehension. Their neighbours argued, divided as to what was best, and in the end the officials in their government cars went away to make the arrangements.

That night the storms started; the winds rattled the shacks and huge waves swept high up the beach. In the morning old Jim and Mr. Peter took their little boat and went to sea.

There was no doubt the shack community would bury their friends and share all costs, however the undertaker would not bury them together. 'It would not be seemly, nor perhaps legal,' he insisted. He could not bury an old man and his old cat in one coffin and one grave no matter the depth of their friendship. The police arrived when tempers began to fray. Taking the city undertaker to one side they spoke persuasively to him, for they had felt the community's love and grieving reaction to the deaths of their own.

Two days later the final ceremony in the sun-dappled bush cemetery was enacted. The shack people stood together and each gently placed a white painted beach stone around the simple grave with the driftwood notice:

JIM AND MR PETER

FRIENDS FOREVER TOGETHER

TWO ROBBERS INTO ONE BANK WON'T GO

Blake (Two Knives) Johnson was tough, anyone could see that. Smooth too – there was a look that people saw even if they didn't know his reputation. Impeccably dressed, black hair sleeked back and a fashionable stubble he could saunter into a bank, a restaurant, anywhere and people gave him respect. You didn't mess with Two Knives and mainly you didn't know where he kept his two knives in his suits. They could just appear like molten mercury in his hands.

This fine August morning Blake was short of cash.

Unusually he'd lost in the casino last night and he wasn't pleased. On impulse he pulled his sports car into the small country town bank to make a withdrawal. At first, they were pleased to see him and wished him a cheery 'Good Morning, Sir.' That was until he pulled one of his namesake knives, the large one, and declined to present his bank card.

Johnno Wilson had one hell of a hangover.

It thundered behind his ears and tightened the skin down the back of his neck. Every push on the pedals of his old bike clamped another round of pain in his head and even his eyeballs hurt. Further he was in trouble. Money troubles when he'd tangled with some old pals and they'd ended up at the casino. Black Jack wasn't his game but a dozen shots of vodka later he'd played as though he knew what he was doing. He didn't, and now he owed money, big money to some low life loan sharks. More money than he'd ever hope to pay back even if he had a job. There was one way out, he thought through the alcohol induced bravado that still feathered his brain, the bank.

Johnno stumbled through the glass doors of the bank and sprawled his length on the black and white marble floor inside. The jolt made him gasp and he crawled to a convenient waste paper bin and threw up a disgusting mess of alcohol and the hamburger he'd eaten at six am. The aroma gushed through the area as he pulled himself to his feet by a teller's booth.

'This is a stickup,' he shouted and wiped his mouth with a gathered bank slip. As he stood there the realization struck that he had no weapon to make such a threat. He thrust the stinking bin towards the teller and she recoiled. 'OK,' he shook the bin, 'You'll get this in your face if you don't hand over some money. All of it,' he added eyeing her money drawer. His adrenalin was pumping and he leaned over the counter, bin first into the woman's space.

A large knife speared the counter near his shoulder. 'You'll get this if you don't get out of here, punk!' The voice was steely and Johnno jolted. He pulled himself upright to stare at this intrusion and blinked as he attempted to focus on the knife now pushing the tip of his nose upwards.

'I'm robbing this bank,' Johnno bravadoed eyes crossed.

'I was here first,' the knife pushed upwards. 'Get out... or better still stand over there until I'm gone.' The knife released his nose and was pointed to where a small group of people who waited and watched. The knife traversed an ark and the people looked away.

Johnno swung around to comply and the contents of the bin still in his hands shifted. They sprayed out flying on the waste paper in the bin and hit Blake Two Knives suit. Bits clung. He swore and lunged at Johnno. Sidestepping amazingly for one so hungover, Johnno decided it was time to vacate the premises. He slipped on his own vomit and slid towards the door. Looking over his shoulder he pushed and pushed the heavy glass door. It wouldn't budge. Panic set in and his pushes got harder, his boot got involved and he kicked at the door. No-one moved although Blake swore. One of the customers suddenly stepped forward and pulled the door open.

Johnno rushed outside and looking around saw the sports car. The key was in the lock and the motor hummed. He leapt in and crashed the gears into third. The car jolted and bucked forward and away around the corner.

Blake Two Knives was now the centre of attention as the staff and the customers looked back towards him. With disgusting muck still clinging to his suit he concluded that robbing this bank was a secondary consideration. He'd already been there too long and the police were probably stirring from their morning coffee to attend this unusual small town event. Getting his car back and dealing with the idiot who stole his car was more important.

'Don't anyone move,' he instructed as he went out onto the quiet street. There were few cars. Nothing that had keys in them. His eyebrows furrowed in distaste as he mounted Johnno's discarded bike and rode off following the sound of grating gears and shrieking tyres, around the corner.

The police sirens shrieked along the street...

REMEMBRANCE DAY PRELUDE

Joel stood alone as the larger boys circled him like a pack of dingoes.

'Resist', he thought. 'Don't react.'

Instinctively he scrunched his body inwards to shield himself, as the taunts grew louder. The first expected jarring pushes came from behind. As usual.

A snarling boy, obviously the leader, jerked Joel's black hair back and glared into his face. 'We don't like people like you,' he threatened almost conversationally.

The victim pulled away. 'Leave me alone,' he implored. 'I've done nothing against you.' His tense words were careful and precise. Exactly what he had been taught in school when dealing with bullies. Try not to show fear. Ask them to stop. 'Nothing.''

'Nothing? You exist! You spoil our school with your scholarships. You're scum!' The boy looked around for agreement from his circling group then he jerked the boy's shoulder hard. The grey school uniform fabric of the shirt ripped sharply at the seams as the sound the school bell echoed across the grounds. He pushed Joel away and sauntered off to their next class. His dismissal of the smaller boy was as punishing as his words and actions.

'The Anzac Day commemorations tomorrow morning will begin at 10.30. We'll march out to the ceremony beginning at 10.45,' the teacher reminded the class next day. 'Those of you who have brought medals that belonged to your fathers and grandfathers are invited to wear them. It should be a proud day for you to do that and some of you will have your families coming too.'

There was a murmur as the self-appointed class leader, Rex

Bartlett, made a bow in the back of the room. He had already brought his grandfather's Vietnam medals to school and now he held up the service ribbons and medals in his hand. His friends paid tribute – loudly as expected of them.

'You should look after those, Rex,' the teacher admonished. 'They are important both to your family and to Australia.'

Joel sat quietly.

That evening his Nanna sewed up the rip in his shirt. She was quiet for a moment then she went into her room and brought out a small, dented gun-grey metal tin. She placed it carefully on the table.

'This is my special tin,' her voice was soft and although her English was excellent, she still had an Asian accent. She smiled. 'It doesn't look like much, does it?'

Joel shook his head.

'It belonged to my husband, your grandfather. You know he was an American soldier in the Vietnam War?'

'Yes Nanna,' he reverently and he touched the tin.

There was a smile of remembrance in her voice. 'He carried this tin full of peppermints on his missions... but it was the only thing they gave me after he was killed. That and what it contains.'

She opened the tin. Campaign medals glittered. One that Joel recognized by its shape was a Purple Heart. He had heard about them. Another medal lay attached to pale faded blue ribbon with thirteen white stars on a dark blue patch. The large medal had a golden eagle surmounting a large star.

'Can I take these to school for the Anzac Day ceremony?' Joel asked.

'Yes, you can,' his Nanna said. 'Be proud of them. You know your part American and that your grandfather fought there.'

'Yes, Nanna.'

Next day the class lined up ready for the Anzac Day Service. Many children wore medals.

Rex Bartlett charged up to Joel and flicked the medals on his mended shirt. 'Only two medals?' he challenged. 'I've got more than you. You little jerk! I don't know why you bother wearing them at all.' He pulled at the Purple Heart. 'Did you get that one out of a Christmas Cracker?' he scoffed. His cohort laughed, as expected.

Joel looked down at the Purple Heart. It wasn't the most elegant of medals, it shone too brightly and even made the other medal his Nanna had loaned him look pale and insignificant.

'They're American medals,' he admitted.

The bullies chortled. 'American! They're not proper medals. Not Australian medals. They hardly count at all.'

'Come class, form into your lines and we'll march down to the oval where everyone is waiting.' The teacher led the way not knowing that Joel was still being bullied by the other boys. Throughout the flag raising ceremony, the two minutes silence and the playing of the Last Post the boys continued to poke and prod Joel as he stood to attention and tried to follow the message of the day.

'Resist,' he reminded himself as the ceremony ended and the harassment continued.

Joel saw his Nanna sitting quietly; a small figure, grey hair drawn back into a simple knot and wearing a blue cotton dress and sensible sandals. Afterwards the ceremony he went to her.

'I am proud of you,' she said in her precise English. 'You did not respond to those boys... One day you may have to.'

Suddenly a large man strode up and stopped abruptly in front of Joel and Nanna. His dark bearded scowl covered them like a dark blanket. Behind him Joel's nemesis smirked.

The man reached forward as if to touch the boy's chest and medals. Joel crouched and his hands went up instinctively into a defensive position.

'Whoa...!' the man boomed. A grin of understanding spread

across his face.

Joel relaxed his hands down and stood tall again.

'May I?' the man asked.

He stooped and looked closely at Joel's chest. Eyes targeted on the medal with the eagle, he stepped back, straightened, and in front of the school population and his startled grandson Rex, he snapped a smart salute.

'Thank you,' Nanna said quietly. Her Vietnamese eyes glinted with tears under her wide hat.

'That, boys,' the man addressed Rex and his gaping cohort, 'is the American Medal of Honour. It's like the Victoria Cross and there's no higher military medal for bravery in the US forces. All ranks salute it.'

Joel looked around. A circle had formed around them; his teacher, classmates and other parents. People were smiling.

Rex's grandfather held out his hand. 'May I shake your hand?' he asked. They shook.

He turned again to Nanna. 'You must be proud and...,' he said, 'I see also that your boy knows how to defend himself?'

Joel looked at his feet as again Rex and his group gaped.

Nanna stood. 'Yes,' she said. 'He is progressing well in Tae Kwon Do. He has learned the art and knowledge of self discipline.' She faced Rex and his grandfather defiantly. 'Others could do the same...'

'Yes,' the old soldier said and his own gaze turned menacingly towards his grandson and his friends. 'I saw...and my grandson will have his education amended forthwith.'

K.I.S.S. – R.I.P.

I awoke in the Adelaide summer pre-dawn.

After tossing on satin sheets for most of the night I'd finally made up my mind. Eric Petersen had to die and I'd kill him. I switched on the overhead-ceiling fan and luxuriated in the draft of air that licked about my body. Yes, but there would be problems. Lots of problems. Especially in a city like Adelaide; a small city, an overgrown country town where everyone knew each other. Everyone who mattered.

The major one – Eric. He was a police detective, a good cop. The prototype tall blond all-round wholesome guy. So good in fact he'd become a bore and our relationship had deteriorated. Well, from my perspective anyway. We'd been together for four years. Initially the interaction between us had crackled. I knew every nuance of Eric's character, and his body as well for that matter. We'd shared everything. The day and night shifts, midnight stakeouts watching drug deals go down on Hindley Street and long days in the courts listening to the drone of lawyers. It'd been enough to keep a woman intrigued.

For a while.

Now Eric was beginning to show interest in other women. There are always women in police cases and they flirted with him. Openly. He cast a speculative eye in their direction too. I knew. I'm a curvy brunette with a rapid-fire temperament and if one of us was approaching the 'use by date' in the relationship. It wasn't going to be me.

Also, I fancied someone new.

In Rocco I'd found what I was looking for. Just thinking about him; the garlic and chillies, the man smell, make me tingle. Mastering him promised to be delicious. His undercover beat covered criminal bikey haunts, the mean pubs and smoky bars. Rocco shrugged into gang leathers and walked easy on the dirty pavements where rock and rap thumped through the bones or jazz leaked out of dark doorways like water to form puddles in the gutters. A Harley motor bike was an extension of his long legs and steel capped boots. He fitted the shadows and sought the unexpected.

Like me he knew when to throw out society's mores and the rulebooks.

Already it was hot and the morning gasped for breath as the illusion of coolness dissipated with the light. Finally, I got out of bed and wandered into the shower. I needed the cold waters to get my mind working this morning. I knew Eric's caseload. I knew where he would be every moment and, as his controller, I could determine the time and place where a fatal 'incident' could happen.

I deliberated. Poison – the women's weapon? Too predictable. Too boring. A revenge or contract killing? Road rage? A police case gone wrong? Things happen when you're on the beat. The idea of a knife slipping between his ribs and a surprised look on his face was appealing. Not quite my style though. Maybe get someone else to do the job? No, I decided – it could get out of my hands.

I like to be in control.

I knew I couldn't get any of the other police to help. Even those who would like to take his place with me. I'd had offers. Plenty! No, I wanted to come out of with my reputation intact. Pouting into the bathroom mirror I wondered, hypothetically, how I'd look in black widow's weeds. Maybe that would be going a bit too far. There was a delicious badness in deciding how to murder Eric.

'KISS – Keep It Simple Stupid', I decided. Keep it sweet. I plotted and set it up. No time like the present. The timing, yes, around midnight on another sweltering night when the world huddled in on itself and flared with irritable temper. A night when violence was not unexpected.

It suited the mood and the act.

Eric was on the graveyard shift and, forever grumbling, he'd keyed a lengthy report into the computer. He stretched and announced to the nearly empty squad room that he was going out to get a snack at an all night cafe. Eric'd have gone to the old Pie Cart by the Railway Station if it was still going but instead he grabbed his keys and left. I gave him time to get his hamburger then radioed him to go to our rendezvous spot beside the Torrens River. Check out a simple matter. Someone reported loitering. Our password. We'd met before like this for a little erotic relaxation on our meal breaks.

It used to be fun.

Eric went eagerly, unsuspecting trouble and waited in the shadows where the moon seemed connected to the river banks by a long silver pathway. Always beautiful. Before he could register delight much less surprise at seeing me with a gun – I pulled the trigger. No regrets. No witnesses. Gloved – no DNA on the gun I'd found years ago and hadn't bothered to register. I left him messy with the burger and salad all over him. Nice touch. Then I threw the gun into the black deep muddy mid-river channel. Returned. Clean.

The investigation I set up was simple really. I'm very efficient. The case remained unsolved for lack of tangible evidence. Too many past cases provided countless motives and suspects. An 'open' coroner's verdict. Then the long procession of police vehicles winding through the Adelaide streets and lights flashing for Eric. Eulogies at the police funeral and his hat resting on the coffin. Sad really.

Now Rocco! I could hardly wait!

A good night's work! It made a woman hungry. I telephoned for sun-dried tomato and garlic pasta. Delivered. My fingers traced a satisfied path along the line of four, soon to be five, 'ERIC PETERSEN' books. With a tiny, even regretful, sigh I typed 'R.I.P. THE END' on the final page of 'R.I.P. – GOODBYE' and filed dear Eric on computer disc for my publisher.

I smiled as I opened a new file...

BLACK MOON SETTING

'I am the clone...' the ancient crone said matter of factually, 'of Letishka, the prophetess of the Black Moon of Erlish.' Her blank black eye sockets were magnets for the hundreds of torch fires as her subjects jostled to bow low in her presence. Her eyes drank the lights into her darkness.

He wasn't prepared to argue. All he wanted was the black orb she held in the purple claws that passed for her hands. She wasn't human and, clone of Letishka or not, he didn't care.

Tonight, the moon above was edging to the black she alluded to as it sank towards the splintered mountain range in the north. He had no inkling of the what, or the why, of the ceremony was she was conducting within the stone monoliths. It didn't matter but he knew he had to act fast, now, before the moon was gone.

His quest was to get that ambergris orb and if he had to steal it, then so be it.

She held the orb tight to her bent body and her towering costume head-dress bowed over it as he pushed through the crowd and stretched his hands to snatch the prize from her. With one razor tipped hand she parried his grasp and thrust it against his chest. The claws dug in and he was stopped in excruciating pain as they and each probe wrapped around his heart. Slowly she raised her head and the ugly mask-face looked at and through him.

'I am the clone of Letishka,' she repeated and the claw hand twisted inside him. His hands, still clutching towards the orb, dropped to his side and she released his heart and shook her hand free of his alien presence. He fell to the stone pathway – every wit of energy drawn out.

There was no blood.

'You will wait,' she instructed, standing straight now, her head-dress gleaming as the black moonlight crippled the planet's natural glow. As he lay spread where he had fallen, he saw her throng of beings, inch forward to touch her and she received their adulation now as a tall and beautiful being.

Strident sounds engulfed him to unconsciousness.

When he woke the Black Moon had set and he held the precious orb in his claws. 'I am the clone of...' he screamed into the barren black dawn.

THE MAGIC BUTTON

I discovered the magic button on my shirt quite by accident.

You know the shirt, the blue one I wear almost daily until, I'll bet, everyone thinks I own nothing else. The button looks like all the rest and the other buttons just well, button up my shirt, but the second button – that's special.

OK – I'll go back to the beginning.

I bought this shirt, almost new, from an op shop. It had once been a very expensive shirt but I got it for a few dollars. I took it home, and washed it to wear it next day. But what I hadn't noticed, when I bought the shirt, was there was one button missing. There's nothing unusual about that, is there? Not when you buy an op shop shirt.

That's when things began to get interesting after a rather sad time for me.

Again, I'll need to explain.

I lived with my Nanna after my parents died when I was six. Dear old Nanna became my parents, my friend, my confidant, and most of all she was fun. But a few months ago, just after my thirtieth birthday and, me still a bachelor, Nanna died. Suddenly and without fuss. Nanna's way. I missed her terribly but tried to get on with my life, to get things back to normal, as she would have wished. A daily walk on the beach became a pleasant time to think and to ground myself. Often I felt her presence. A good feeling and I'd mentally have a chat discussing daily things with her as if she was still with me.

The morning after I discovered that I had a missing button I spotted, of all things, a blue button washing up with the shells and sea weed on the high tide line of our favourite beach.

'Pick it up,' a thought in Nanna's voice instructed. 'That's a perfect match for the missing shirt button.'

'What a lucky coincidence,' I agreed and picked it up. Now I'm not much with a needle and thread but after work that night, I sewed the button onto my shirt as best I could. I smiled as I tugged at the last stitch. Nanna would have approved.

Things changed next morning. As I was buttoning up my new shirt I thought, 'I'd better do some washing...' Also rather guiltily, 'and do some other chores about the house.'

Everything happened at once!

The clothes washing machine filled itself and started churning away. Empty!

The dishwasher started – almost empty and the vacuum cleaner charged out of the cupboard and began cleaning the carpet. I rushed around turning everything off and cussed impatiently about the waste of water and electricity. A few minutes later as I took my first sip of breakfast coffee the machines started again. I thrust a load of washing into the determined washing machine and turned the other appliances off – twice. Twice before they got the message to stay off!

'What's the matter with electrical stuff today?' I said aloud. Maybe we were getting surges down the electricity lines.

I gave no thought to the button. Not then!

My breakfast coffee was cold by now. I sat grumpily at the table and idly contemplated what to make for dinner. Now I realise that I must have touched the button again. Or spoken aloud. Living alone, I was talking to myself a lot since Nanna died.

Suddenly the freezer door burst open. A tray of frozen lamb chops flew out, the gas stove turned on, and the chops, plastic wrapper and all, popped in under the griller flame. As I stared stunned two potatoes bounced out of the pantry, flew past my head onto the kitchen sink, and a saucepan clattered inside the closed drawer as if it were trying to get out. My knife jumped off the knife block and rattled loudly as though calling for me to start peeling. The fridge door opened and whiz, carrots and beans followed and arranged themselves beside the potatoes. Apparently, I was having chops and vegies for dinner if I could get the melting plastic off the chops that were already sizzling. I hit the OFF button on the grill, threw the hot chops into the sink and scuttled back to my chair.

I sat there too bewildered to move. Visions of a haunted house rattled around in my brain and I must have smoothed down my shirt in agitation.

A damp flannel charged out of the bathroom and arranged itself on my forehead. I pushed it away and it fell on the floor. The cloth picked itself up and flew back to the bathroom to rewash itself. Again it placed itself on my brow just like Nanna used to do when I was upset or hurt as a child. 'Is this expected to calm me?' I wondered. It did, surprisingly, and as though given the thought, I touched the buttons on my shirt.

The second button felt warm, smoother and seemed to melt invitingly into my fingers. I felt an immediate link with Nanna.

'I really needed another cup of coffee', I thought, and tentatively I stroked the blue button. Nothing happened. Then it hit me and I laughed out loud. Nanna drank tea, tea only, and she said she couldn't make a decent cup of coffee. Or wouldn't. 'Make your own,' she'd insist, her smile hovering around her mouth. 'The proper drink for a refined gentleman is tea.'

'So!' I determined. 'Maybe you're still around, old girl, but why have you taken so long to show yourself?'

Nanna had hoped that I would marry one day but with my physiotherapy practice, sport, my hobbies, and some charity work, I'd never found the time, nor the right person. Maybe she had given up on me and decided that I needed something else to help me through the lonely days ahead.

But send me a magic button? OK, but now I just had to find out how to make the magic button work. Maybe it could be useful, fun even. I turned to the shirt and peered at the button and under it. No instructions. I'm not sure where I would have found instructions but, coffeeless and as you can imagine, I was not thinking very clearly.

I sat there perplexed.

Slowly a smile came. That clever old woman, I thought, sending me a magic button to keep me on my toes. I've learned a few of the magic button's tricks; some are useful and many work in hilarious ways.

Then a week later on a Saturday morning, just after I'd got home from helping with the local school's football team, my doorbell rang.

At the door was Liz, a young lady from my adult bookbinding class. She staggered under the weight of the huge bundle of used children's story books she carried.

'These need restoring for the overseas orphan's school,' she said. 'You did say that this Saturday morning would be convenient for me to drop them off, didn't you? Maybe we could repair them together?'

I looked blankly at her. Sometimes bachelors are forgetful and a lot had been happening over the last few days.

Then I remembered we'd talked on the phone.

On the phone at home. And I'd been wearing that blue shirt.

'Great,' I stammered. 'Come on in. Have a cup of tea with me.'

I touched my magic button. Immediately from the kitchen I heard the gentle rattle of china and teaspoons. The kettle pinged.

The books in her arms started to slip sideways.

'Whoa there!' I steadied them, then remembering my manners after my confusion at finding Liz on my doorstep; I took the bundle from her. 'The kettle's hot,' I said confidently.

'Are you sure you have time?' Liz asked, 'and would you mind if I had a coffee?' Her smile lit up her face.

What a gorgeous face, I thought.

Wow, Liz looked different now from the night class. Usually she appeared as the local librarian but this morning she looked modern and trendy. Her dark hair was a mass of loose curls and she had warm dark brown eyes. No rings on her fingers, I noted.

I suddenly realised that my book-worm Nanna would have known Liz from her weekly library visits.

'Yes, I'm very sure.' I touched the magic button again. 'I think I have some nice shortbread biscuits too,' I said.

Then it hit me. She'd asked for coffee.

Hmmm…? The button making coffee?

Immediately I heard the sound of biscuit wrapping being opened in the kitchen and then biscuits sliding onto a plate. The smell of fresh brewed coffee wafted down the hallway.

'Come in…' I invited grinning now. 'Coffee'll be ready in just a minute.'

Crafty old Nanna! Her and her magic blue button!

If she were playing Cupid – I was ready to see what happened next.

SOLITAIRE IN DIAMONDS

Black and red the Solitaire cards lay before Maggie on the computer screen. She swirled the mouse in irritation on her desk pad then diminished the card game to the lower tool bar. With a frown she maximised the screen that was the real reason for her on going conjecture.

'WANTED', it read.

'American national Raymond Blight wanted in connection with the theft of 15 kilograms of gem and industrial grade diamonds from Argyle Mines, Western Australia. Estimated value $100,000,000.00. Substantial reward offered for information leading to the return of the diamonds and the conviction of the offender.'

The passport photo displayed on the screen was indistinct.

She frowned in annoyance. Couldn't they get a better reproduction of a passport, she thought.

The person was male. Dark haired and swarthy in complexion. Early forties. This passport could be dodgy, just the poor photo quality made her suspicious.

The general consensus of police investigation was that Raymond Blight and the diamonds were well out of Australia. Probably taken by fast motorboat off one of the long, lonely beaches on the West Coast. There was a follow up note in the report that a few of the stones, discernible by individual geological structure of minerals worldwide, had turned up abroad. Maggie's immediate though was that a few stones could be mailed to an accomplice to provide the readies for getting the main diamond cargo out. It was six months since the robbery and maybe things were still too hot to try yet.

Maggie flicked back to the card game and stared into the screen as her hand automatically clicked the cards.

Black on red.

Red on black.

A uniformed Police Officer, Gary Leigh, put his head around the doorway and saw the card game. 'Got a problem, Detective Sergeant?' he questioned with a broad smile.

Maggie gave a rueful chuckle.

'Yeah! This...' she said as she flicked back to the 'Wanted' notice. She looked up at Gary now with a returning grin. Playing computer card games was her idiosyncrasy, and the one despite her rank, she was teased about. But she got results and they had learned to accept her methods. In her mid 30's Maggie had built a solid reputation of good leadership and fine investigative work. The country senior posting was her reward although she knew she was still faced with the inevitable 'glass ceiling' still hanging above all female detectives' heads.

Gary gestured towards the screen. 'You reckon you know who and where he is? And the sparklers?'

'Yeah, I think I know the who is. And I'll find a way to prove it. Get the diamonds back too.' She pushed back a strand of hair that had escaped from her mane of dark curls to behind her ear as she flicked back to the card game. 'Maybe this isn't the accepted way to solve crime. Sometimes it helps.' She smiled, 'Lets the subconscious run free. '

Gary kept a straight face, almost. 'Yeah, sure...'

'What else have you got for me? Finished your final report on the car thieves yet? Good work on that by the way Gary. I've noted your observations in my investigation.'

'Thanks for that. We've had a call from a farmer. He reckons that a couple of sheep have gone missing. Not foxes either. Happens this time of year as the market lamb prices get better.'

'OK get onto it. And keep me informed. I'm going to go over something and I need to do it today...'

'Sure. Will do'

Gary left then poked his head back around her door. You going to Sam's wine launch tonight?'

'We've been friends for years. Wouldn't miss it.'

'Pity, I'm on duty tonight.'

'I'll have a glass for you then. It'll be a good show.'

Maggie swung out of her chair. She smiled again at the thought of the evening ahead. Being with Sam was always wonderful. But now she needed more coffee. Even the instant rubbish that was provided in the tiny kitchen outside in the squad room was better than nothing.

She stopped as she passed the office window. Outside a spring shower chased a shaft of sunlight across grape vines on the hill slopes above the town. They were already pruned and waiting for the late rains and warmer weather, after the sub-zero chill of winter nights, and to cause new green shoots to shrug clear of the brown canes.

She looked down into the car compound below the window. Great, forensics had finished fingerprinting her car, and Danny's. They would both get them back today. Danny Nevada was Sam's financial business partner, and getting the car back represented a

triumph for her when it could have been an embarrassment. Or a disaster.

There had been a spate of car thefts in her region, not the usual hotted up eight cylinders vehicles, but good cars taken. That was when she had professional contact with Danny Nevada. He reported, angrily and often, that his new diesel Mercedes sports car had been stolen. That was three weeks ago. Maggie and her crew had investigated without much luck and she and Danny had continued their veiled, but mutual dislike of each other.

But then the thieves made a mistake.

They targeted Maggie's own old Merc; her pride and joy. Targeted it in her driveway one night. She was just about go to put rubbish in the recycle bin when she heard someone trying to start the engine. Her response had been immediate and she grabbed the man with his head under the car bonnet in a professional grip and had him cuffed before he knew what hit him. It was an instant cop and the thief had sung immediately as they did when Maggie's eyes bored into them.

In the interview room Gary Leigh had noted that the thief's sneakers were covered in grease as well as mud and Maggie contacted the forensics branch. Within days they had matched the grease with the muck on the floor of a rented farm garage, perfect evidence to add to the recovery of three stolen vehicles, including Danny Nevada's car.

What had sparked Maggie's nose again for the suspicious was, after all his fuss when the car was stolen, Danny had hardly acknowledged that he had got it back intact. On an impulse Maggie asked a favour of forensics for a complete check on the car; they did it but reported nothing amiss.

It just didn't jell.

It was as though the car didn't matter anymore.

She had tried to get a reaction, as a fellow Mercedes owner, that his diesel took longer to start than her old petrol engine did. With distain he refrained from rising to the bait she cast.

'Just let me know when I can pick up the car. I'm a busy man with the export planned for tomorrow and Sam's wine launch tonight. You're coming I suppose?' The last remark was less than an invitation.

'Yes, of course...'

'Well, I need the car before then.' Danny's interruption was abrupt. A total dismissal.

When Danny reported his car missing Maggie had taken the opportunity to do all the checks possible on him. Passport, nationality, car registration and licence. Past offences in Australia. He'd been in the country for just over a year, in Western Australia she'd traced that, but it was as though he didn't exist before then. That started her mind to link him with the diamonds. She'd played her hunch but all her computer queries had come up negative. It was infuriating.

Coffee finally in hand, Maggie returned to her desk and computer screen. The cards spread before her as she sipped.

She muttered. 'I know it's him, dammit, but how's he getting the diamonds out of Australia?'

Discretely while visiting Sam at the vineyard, she had managed a check of the packing cases the wine bottles would be transported in. They looked completely innocent.

Like the card array the 'how' evidence was elusive. Hidden. Waiting for the right card to be played. She wanted that card.

Maggie needed a breakthrough at Sam's launch. Her professional instincts told her it could be too late after that.

Tonight was the key.

Sam's vineyard was different, just as Sam was different. He was a widower who had successfully raised a son, Peter, from a baby while establishing himself as an inspired wine maker. He made white table wines as his special preference even though his boutique wine company produced robust reds. He was also an enthusiast of native vegetation and liked red native bottlebrush and had planted them around his vines in glorious scarlet profusion. Local winemaker opinion was that the Callistemon could affect the nose of his grapes but, defiantly, Sam ascertained the vibrancy was an asset. His new label, 'Down Under Riesling', featured the full-headed red flowers as his logo.

The evening air was spring soft for the wine launch. The day's rain showers had spruced up the clipped lawn and freshened the air. A nearly full moon flooded the area and a magpie, sitting on a high tree branch, filled its throat and scat a melody of liquid jazz along the hills. Crowds gathered on the grass between banks of display wines and the scarlet echo of bottlebrush bushes.

White clothed tables were spread with accompaniments of cheeses and breads and already an appreciative murmur of voices ebbed and flowed. A gentle breeze that was just enough to add a whisper to the foliage and a ruffle of perfume from the red flowers. The setting was perfect as Sam had carefully planned and his superb Riesling splashed gently golden into the waiting sparkling glasses.

Danny Nevada rolled tiny stones in his tuxedo pocket. They matched too – pale gold and dazzling white. His plans were working. Scornfully he observed as Maggie pulled into a parking space in her small Merc. She didn't look too bad tonight! Off duty and a much different presence. Gone were the smart casual clothing of the detective and she was decidedly glamorous in a black cocktail dress. Her dark hair was loose and there was even a glitter of tiny diamonds in her ears. He carefully ignored her ever watchful eyes, as his smile of greeting played only about his mouth. One insolent hand remained in his pocket.

'Evening Maggie.'

Danny let his eyes do a wander from the top of her curls to the toes of her killer stilettos. He raised an apparently appreciative eyebrow.

Maggie carefully returned his greeting. 'Good evening, Mr Danny Nevada,' she said. He noted her formality in using his whole name conveying, as usual, that to her, even his name was dubious. He knew he was an enigma to her and he enjoyed flouting his confidence. Her reservations about him were a challenge.

Tonight, would be his final moments in the vineyard and Danny almost laughed out loud. He smiled again at her before turning away and genially returned greetings and congratulations from other patrons milling around.

Danny Nevada played the perfect host.

Sam smiled, raised a hand in greeting at Maggie from across the lawns, and started towards her before he was cornered by two wine critics from a city paper. He managed to shrug another smile before waiting for their verdicts. This was business. Critics were important for future sales.

But first, David, raised his glass of white wine to Sam.

'This has it all. Aromas of floral and lime to delight the senses.' He sipped appreciably. 'A lively, acidic palate with citrus and apple that lingers on the tongue. It's an excellent wine. Very commercial.'

'Thank you. So you'll recommend it?' Sam was careful, they could say one thing and write another.

'Absolutely!' David gestured to the crowd. 'Ask anyone here.'

'Have you tried Sam's red?' The second wine critic butted in. 'Sam – it's gorgeous! I tried it earlier. It's so red it's almost purple. I can taste the spicy cherry and plum aromas.' He swirled the white wine in his glass. 'This's good too.'

'You've done wonderfully well for someone with their first vintage.'

Sam laughed. 'This Riesling is new, as you well know, but I've been making red's for quite a while. I've been lucky.'

David protested. 'No, luck is only part of it. You've the skill to make these fabulous wines and luck's just that you've got a financial sponsor to export overseas.'

Danny, hearing the opportunity to impress, sauntered over.

'Yes. You've met Danny Nevada, my business partner?' Sam obliged.

'No, I haven't had that pleasure. I must congratulate him too. He's made a wise investment supporting you.'

'The pleasure was all mine,' Danny oozed.

Sam accepted a fresh glass from Peter, who was passing with a tray and gestured for him to top up the wine critic's glasses.

Tonight, Maggie's concentration was mostly business, but her interest in Sam were very personal. She stood back and took a moment to watch him as he talked to the wine critics. God, he was gorgeous. He suited up well, his face looked lived in and his whole persona was open as he glanced over at her again. Even from the distance between them she sensed his eyes dilated in appreciation of her. It was enough to send a tingle through her body that wasn't attributable to the breeze or her bare shoulders.

Tonight, she looked good and she knew it.

They'd both been made wary by past relationships and losses. Maggie, through her work necessity, had fostered a public and private separateness with the local people. Until she met Sam… They enjoyed each other's quirky cynical humour and dined regularly in local restaurants. They walked and laughed as the friendship sweetened, grew and trusted developed.

Then the mercurial American had appeared at the cellar door one afternoon. He was the essence of charm, enthusiastic about the wines and this was just the wine he wanted to export to the States, he'd said. Everything was just fine until the end of that first day when he found out she was police. After that he dominated Sam's time, his actions and began the exclusion of others. Especially Maggie. If they had a date planned suddenly there was something that only Sam could rectify and Maggie, after dismissing the notion that maybe there was a jealously, she needed to acknowledge, became more and more wary of Danny's motive for financing Sam's export venture. It juxtaposed with the feeling that somehow, he was using Sam.

Tonight, Maggie watched knowing something was wrong. Instinctively wrong.

The last cards still wouldn't fall…

The crowd was larger than expected. Peter, home from uni for the night acted proudly as one of Sam's servers, had added more wine bottles to the chilling fridges in the 'back stage' neat work area. Peter had pulled bottles out of the boxes from the displays.

Unknown to him there were differences in the wine labels. The domestic labels featured a single bottlebrush. The export labels had triple blooms although there was no difference in the wine.

Danny's idea.

Danny's instigation. 'They would appeal more to the US market,' he said. More representative of Australia. Sam knew; he'd even mentioned it to Maggie, but accepted it as a sponsor's knowledge of the market. Danny's fancy.

In his haste Peter chilled both. Peter's eyes were on his girlfriend Fran who was also serving tonight. Laughing flirting Fran. He didn't bother to ask about the wine he served, and he didn't notice the difference. He opened another bottle and began to refill glasses.

Danny sipped from his glass as Peter, wine bottle in hand, moved past him to serve another waiting couple. Danny missed little. He tensed then moved in. Grandly he took the bottle from Peter, and with a flourish held it to the light.

'This bottle's nearly empty,' he admonished Peter. 'We'll get a new one for these fine people.' His accent was mellow as southern velvet and the couple smiled under his personal attention.

Peter shrugged. It was no worry to him. He followed Danny to the cooling area. There Danny turned on him.

'Where'd you get this bottle?' he hissed, the soft accent gone.

Startled Peter pointed to the bottle case he had opened.

'There...' he started.

Danny slammed down the bottle he held and snatched up a single flower labelled bottle from the cooling fridge.

'Get this out to those people,' he snarled, 'and only take the bottles I put in the fridges in future,' he sharply instructed. 'You'd better tell Fran too. Understand?'

Peter uncorked the new bottle while Danny fumed. 'Sorry...I didn't know ....'

'If you spent less time mooning over that blonde bird you'd

know these things,' Danny spat back at him. 'Get back out there!'

Peter picked up his tray and left to continue serving.

Sam strode into the back area. 'It's going well…' he called to Danny. Tonight, he was appreciative of Danny's smooth public charms.

'Yes, but tell …' Danny started.

Peter picked up the nearly empty bottle and refilled his own glass then responded to a voice calling from outside the pavilion. Before Danny could stop him, he was gone. The bottle he had retrieved was now empty.

Danny swore. Eyes hard. He picked up the bottle and, as he saw Maggie enter the area, he abruptly stowed it with the other empties. This was not the time to start to draw attention to the wine bottles.

Maggie was watching. Ever so casually.

'Can I get you another drink?' Danny asked careful again to resume his public persona – especially with Maggie. He felt secure, but even with success so close he could not afford to antagonise this policewoman. 'Or are you on duty?' he challenged. His smile was condescending. Superior.

'No thanks. I'm just looking for Sam,' Maggie replied. Her dark eyes got darker as she levelled a straight look at him.

She started for the door again then turned back, 'Great success tonight,' she said.

For Sam's sake she meant it.

Outside Sam stood nearby. He smiled hugely at Maggie and took her arm.

'I'm a bit worried that I'll have a bit too much of my own wine. I need to drink with everyone,' he confided. Sam quickly emptied his glass into Maggie's empty one. 'You should finish this. Can't waste it.'

He watched while Maggie sipped. She liked his wines and was always appreciative.

'Hmmm...' she said. Her eyes on his above her glass in a moment of intimacy. 'Hmmm...'

She coughed and wide-eyed swallowed.

Sam looked concerned.

Bells rang in her head!

The final solitaire card flipped.

'Yes! Yes! Yes!' Maggie wanted to shout. 'Got you! I've bloody got you!' Without fuss Maggie disengaged herself from Sam as other guests came towards them.

'See you afterwards?' Sam whispered.

Maggie nodded a smile and found a quiet corner. She reached into her small bag, found her mobile phone and called for police backup; then she went inside to confront Danny.

Danny was still in the wine room and was carefully resorting the bottles. The export stack stood tall, probably forty boxes of wine waited to be loaded onto the trucks in the morning. Three or more boxes were open.

Maggie picked up a bottle, a three scarlet bottlebrush labelled one from an open box, her action quickly casual before he could stop her.

She held it admiringly up to the light. 'Gorgeous colour,' she said.

Nothing.

She didn't expect to see anything. Clever, very clever.

Why, O why, hadn't she thought of it earlier?

'That's an export bottle. Shouldn't have been served tonight. I'll have to reseal all the opened boxes now.' Danny's tone was irritated as though this was just a nuisance. He thrust out a hand. 'Give it here.' It was an order. There was no please.

Maggie thought quickly. She needed to get this bottle checked. To break a bottle. She started as though to pass to him but let it slip through her hands. It fell to the floor; the clean concrete floor of the work shed. It didn't smash.

'Damn!' The mild expletive slipped out. She bent and reached for the bottle, getting there before Danny did.

'Leave it!'

'Not likely…' Maggie grasped the body of the bottle and rapped the neck hard on the floor. The top shattered off. Glass went everywhere across the smooth surface. She stood and poured the rest of the pale wine onto a serving tray.

'What the hell do you think you are doing?' Danny yelled. 'Give me that…'

'Not likely,' Maggie repeated.

'Stupid woman! You'll just cut yourself on the glass. Give it to me.' He attempted to shoulder her aside.

'Stand clear! Now!' Maggie instructed in a full police parade ground voice.

He stopped.

Maggie ran her hand through the wetness of the wine remaining on the tray. A glass shard pricked her finger. Though concentrating on the wine in the tray she sensed Danny move.

Maggie looked toward him. 'I want to talk to you,' she said sternly. 'Wait…'

But Danny was off and running out the far door towards the parking area. He was fast and Maggie stood momentarily flat footed. She took off after him with remarkable speed in her high heels.

Danny's hurried feet scattered the carefully raked gravel of the path. He reached his car and Maggie heard the noise of a car door slamming. There was a pause before the diesel engine car started.

'Gives me a few seconds…' Maggie thought as she ran.

The car revved wildly and took off. Stones hit the side of the wine shed. There was a loud metallic screech and a thump. The diesel roared again then there was another sound of rending metal. A splutter of stalled engine.

Silence…

Maggie rounded the corner to see that Danny's expensive car had hit a metal rubbish bin. Crumpled, the bin body was tangled up under the car. The rear wheels were off the ground, spinning uselessly. The rubbish bin lid, impact flung also lay spinning. It caught the lights. Flash. Flashing.

Maggie sprinted down the track and wrenched open the driver's door. Danny looked rumpled and blood leaked down his face from a small cut above his right eye. He sat back stunned, more so as he peered into the business end of Maggie's small personal revolver. He slumped.

A second set of lights flashed; police car lights in red and blue.

'Busy Ma'am?' Gary asked as he pulled up.

'Get him out!' Maggie tried not to puff in the excitement of the chase and capture.

'Yes, Ma'am!'

'Cuff him and get me some gloves,' she said.

Sam and many of the guests arrived. Shock registered across faces as Danny was hand cuffed.

'What's going on?' Sam demanded.

'Crime scene tapes, Boss?' Gary asked. 'Do I call in the team?'

'Yes please. Call in as many as you can. We're going to need a massive amount of security.'

'What...?' Sam's voice was incredulous.

'Bring him back to the brighter lights,' Maggie ordered with a shrug towards Danny.

'The party's over, Sam, and you're about to lose all your export bottles. Sorry.' Maggie was direct and firm when they were all back in the packing area.

'Tell me! What just happened?'

She put on the evidence gloves Gary offered.

Looking dazed and sullen at the hand-cuffs, Danny was abruptly pushed onto a plastic chair.

'What?' Again from Sam.

Maggie, making sure that all present could witness, ceremoniously picked out a three flowered white wine bottle from the export stack.

'Uncork this please,' she said to Gary.

She took a clean table-cloth from a neat pile of spares and made a well using a wine bucket. Then despite an intake of breath from Sam, who was showing angry signs that he was beginning to understand that something bad had happened to his wine, Maggie poured the whole bottle of wine into the depression.

A sludge of pure white and yellow diamonds, like soapy bubble pebbles, emerged as the wine drained.

'They're just quartz. White and yellow quartz bits,' Fran whispered to Peter.

'Whatever the stuff is it's contaminated Dad's wine.'

'No,' Maggie overheard. 'These are first quality uncut diamonds from Argyle.'

'Wow!' breathed Fran.

Maggie picked out another bottle, held it to the light.

'I can't see anything,' Sam insisted.

'There's nothing to see. The stones are clear in the golden wine.' She tipped the bottle and the wine flowed onto the cloth in the bucket.

More diamond pebbles.

'There's probably a small handful of diamonds in each export bottle,' she said. 'And we could have the better part of a hundred million dollars worth here. You may just find yourself with one hell of a reward.'

There was a gasp from the people who crowded as close as Gary would allow.

Maggie turned back to Danny Nevada, nodded, and Gary pulled him to his feet. Within seconds she had the tiny golden rough diamonds from Danny's pocket. Further evidence to tie him up ready for the courts and prison.

'Bitch...' Danny glowered.

Sam raised an eyebrow. 'How did you know...?' he began.

'I've been suspicious of Danny for a while. Just had to find out why and for what.' The detective allowed herself a small laugh. 'And I not only found, but swallowed, the major deception and these...' she put the diamonds from Danny's pocket into an evidence bag, 'will match beautifully with the diamonds in the export wine bottles,' she said.

'Was that it?' Sam asked.

'I knew he was hiding something special as soon as I saw him tonight. One doesn't spoil the line of an Armani tux by putting one's hands in the pockets. It's not done...'

Maggie's voice became firm. 'Raymond Blight or Danny Nevada, or whoever you are – you're under arrest for grand larceny.'

Game over!

Screen full of cascading cards! Solitaire in Diamonds.

DOUGLAS'S BIRTHDAY CARD

Douglas raised his tin cup. 'Cheers!' he called to the stars and the planets, all old friends. Venus in its yellow orb majesty had risen and trailed after red Mars, already high overhead. The desert night was clear and cold. Stars floated, scattered like chunks of white ice across the indigo-black puddle of sky, so close that Douglas could almost grab them to put in his whisky. That is if an Scotsman would desecrate his good whisky with ice.

He saluted them again and took another sip of his whisky. 'Careful,' he cautioned himself as, resettling in his swag, he came perilously close to spilling the golden liquid. 'Got to leave some for tomorrow – it's my birthday tomorrow,' he said aloud, a lonely and stubborn man talking to himself. His audience the low embers of his camp fire and the inland desert an empty painted canvas spread out rumpled and creased to the horizon.

Away off a dingo howled waiting for the moon.

Douglas raised himself on one elbow. His tin cup wobbled. 'Dratted animal!' he said and cursed it graphically. 'Be off with yer!' His slurred shout dissipated quickly into the darkness.

The dingo howled again ending the yowl in a throaty cough.

Very close, behind him.

Douglas steadied. This was an old animal, almost as old as he was, almost as old as he felt. Friend or foe he had never decided. Like his conscience the dingo was always out there. A shadow. Douglas had never seen it. He knew it was watching him, he felt it, but he never quite managed to see it. Often, he'd turned quickly but always it edged away behind the ridges. Usually in the daylight he charged in the dingo's general direction, fists windmilling like he was an inept pub brawler, throwing rocks and shouting hard curses to speed the retreating phantom heels. Sure he felt a fool but he knew it was out there. He knew and he had to be boss in the day.

But the nights were different.

The dingo owned the dark.

Now Douglas resisted the impulse to turn towards the repeated howl and cough that sounded like a man who had smoked hard tobacco all his life. If he moved he knew the animal would slip, flowing like amber oil, down from the red sand crest and meld into the star cast shadows of his mineshafts. He shuddered as the feral presence sounds sent a wave of tremor down his back and his tatty denim collar pressed stiffly into his neck.

The warmth seeped out of his whisky.

Muttering he slumped down again beside the fire. Then, like a man needing pain, his red caked fingernails reached into his breast pocket, to unfold, fold and refold the sheet of paper so old it no longer rustled. His daughter's words had faded into it but they were black acid etched into his mind.

'By the time you get this...' she had written.

He stopped the recitation as the dingo howled again. Closer yet.

'Mum will have gone for good. She said she was going and she'll do it this time. She's had enough. We all have. Don't come home. No one will be here. Stay with your stupid dreams. They never included us – except for the promises. No one believes in them any more, anyway. If you die down those deep holes of yours no-one would know – or care!'

His mind stalled as always. He knew he deserved it. He chased dreams, always had. His wife Kathryn had been his passion - and the kids. Before he lost his job and the stubborn dreams started. Then his Scot's pride got involved. He couldn't return until he proved himself. Kept his promise of riches. A man always had to prove himself. Even if he damned those he loved as he damned himself.

The dingo moved restlessly awaiting the moon and a stone slid beneath its paws and rattled down the slope. Distracted Douglas instinctively turned his ear to the sound and all movement stopped.

The letter finished relentlessly. 'Stay away…' it demanded and it was signed 'Maggie.'

Now almost fearfully he touched his inner pocket again. Another harder envelope was there, so new it had not had time to conform to the shape of his body. He could feel every insistent corner of it. It was like Maggie's card that had found him five birthdays ago. The one that told him she was getting married and hinted forgiveness in a brutal offhand way. There had been nothing since then and Douglas had convinced himself that the original letter was his destiny; that he had misunderstood her card. Now this year another card had arrived, earlier last month.

Fearful, he had not opened the new card. It glared at him each time he dared to take it from the inner pocket of his coat. The coat that he wore each night against the desert cold and he could feel it and hear the scrape of the envelope against the cloth.

The desert air was chill, the sun long gone. Now the moon, full this night, edged white and cold above the ridges. The dingo, apparently satisfied, circled silently around him and slunk finally in front to where Douglas could see it. He started in shock as yellow eyes reflected briefly in the fire's low glow. He yelled, screaming obscenities and it scuttled away. He held his breath and could hear the soft wash of displaced tailings as it went and he was alone.

The sky crouched lower pressing silence into him. He shuffled his feet disturbing his fire and the embers slumped so softly as though refusing to reassure his ears. Around him the dunes seemed to move in and suddenly he was claustrophobic with loneliness. He reached up and pulled his jacket around his head, cocooning himself.

Against the night. Against time, guilt and place.

Points pricking like skewers the new envelope pressed crisply into his huddled chest. The moon sloped higher providing more light. He straightened himself. Tonight was different. Seeing the dingo for the first time proved that. It was suddenly imperative this night before his birthday to open the envelope. Anything to prove that he still existed. He chucked a lump of wood on the fire then his rough hands pulled the envelope free. Smoothing the face of it, his fingers traced the stamp and they fumbled as he tore the paper open.

As the fire flickered and caught he saw the card showed a seascape. His mouth twisted into the beginnings of a wry smile. Trust Maggie. She'd remembered when they had flown red kites on the long beach with the sea flicking salt spray at them...so long ago...

Two scraps of photographs fell from the envelope.

He fumbled for his lantern, flicked the switch and his campsite lit up. Drab grey tent on red earth and his spare work pants slung over his camp chair. His opal sorting table with his teapot and cup. Everything neatly utilitarian.

The photographs lay face up and he grabbed for the first. It showed a little girl, maybe three years old. A huge grin beamed at him and one small hand reached out in a jaunty 'thumbs up' gesture. She was breathtaking in her fair beauty and she had to be Maggie's daughter. He trembled as he lined up the second photograph on his knee. This was a baby, darker hair feathering on her cheeks and so seriously entranced with a rose she held to be oblivious to the prying camera.

He felt as though he had been punched in the chest as he rocked back and forth looking from one photo to the other. Sweet pain flooded his being and the stale whisky in his system was replaced by euphoria he could not have imagined.

Now he read the card.

'Dad, you stupid old fool,' it began in exasperated salutation. 'You've never answered my last card. Meet your grand daughters, Beth and Zoe. It's time you came home. You're too old to be up there on your own and the kids need a grandfather.'

The card was signed with a flourish by Maggie, there was a pencil scrawl from a baby hand and down in the bottom corner was another small signature. It said simply, 'Love Kathryn.'

Slowly he got to his feet. Douglas's feet instinctively moved into a clumsy jig around his campfire. His hands waved above his head the photos and the card.

'Come out! Come out, wherever you are,' he shouted to the dingo. 'Come and look at this...'

The dingo coughed, still nearby, but did not show itself again.

Next morning the sun poured heat and bush flies over the opal fields. The dingo sat high on the tailings heap. It scratched then lifted its hind leg in rude farewell.

Douglas thumped the steering wheel of his old Land Rover. 'Wish me a happy birthday! You old devil...' he yelled without malice. The dingo loped away and for the first time he confirmed his reasoning that it too was an old male. 'Go home! Home to your bairns,' he shouted as he let out the clutch and the vehicle rattled forward away from the fields. A lifetime of hot colour bulged in his pocket and a tiny jot of fear remained in his being as in the clearer light of day he left to answer the call of the birthday card.

Going home.

THE EMPTY CHAIR

Emily sat alone at the small dining room table in the retirement home her gentle, softly lined face turned towards the empty chair opposite her.

'A little man sat on a chair,
A little man who was not there...'

'Dear Edgar,' she said sweetly, 'at least try this lovely tuna salad.' She paused as though listening. 'Let me put some more salt on it.' She shook the salt shaker above the empty plate, then her smile creases deepened as she whispered, 'Look! I'll put some of your special pepper on it.' She delved into her large worn leather handbag and producing a paper swatch she tapped a smidgin of pepper onto the plate. With that she concentrated on her own salad, occasionally making a comment towards the empty chair. Try as she might Edgar could not be tempted by the apple tart and cream that followed as desert. Emily pouted at the empty chair before she ate hers and lingered over her cup of tea. She fingered the locket containing Edgar's photograph and locks of his hair that lay nestled in the folds of her floral blouse. Finally rising, walking stick in hand, she nodded to the other residents and staff and went back to her room and the afternoon TV programs that awaited her.

The nursing and dining room staff smiled at her daily performance, at her continuing care of her long dead husband. So touching, that setting the extra place at the table for the old devoted, if demented lady, was routine. Only Lyn, a senior nurse in the nursing home, watched with unease. Emily's file certainly showed a failing heart but the tests for dementia, were in her experience and opinion, less than conclusive. Not quite right. One night she told Emily and Edgar's story to her police detective partner Ben, who laughed and said her imagination was working overtime.

A gentleman resident, after inquiring gallantly if he may join her, began to share the small dining table occupied by Emily and the presence of Edgar. Frank, a once tall but now stooped ex army major of ninety summers was a chatty man who made Emily's eyes sparkle and her laugh tinkle. She gently chided both men to eat well, one from a full plate and the other from the ghost meal before the empty chair. Frank seemed charmed as she fussed at each meal time offering napkins, salt and condiments.

Again the staff watched and noted the small gathering and even began to wonder if there could be a little romance happening between Emily and Frank, with Edgar's blessing of course. Lyn watched with the others, aware that the charming Frank's health was failing, as was Emily's heart.

One day all was not right at the cosy table. Emily seemed cross with Edgar. After a burst of angry words directed at him she turned her back on the empty chair and refused to speak to him. As any gentleman would Frank tried to calm the quarrel as if there were two combatants but Emily remained firmly turned away from Edgar and coyly flirted with Frank. The meal was eaten with only Frank receiving her lavish attention. 'Edgar,' Emily scolded the empty chair as she and Frank left the dining room, 'you must not be so jealous.'

Apparently, a truce was called next day and the trio peacefully dined together from then onwards until one day Frank was too ill to attend. He became bedridden and soon died quietly of old age and 'his old war stomach wounds'. Emily was sad and dignified at the loss but after a respectful period of mourning returned to dining in the communal room. She ate again with Edgar as her ghostly companion but had obtained a lock of Frank's hair that she lovingly placed into her locket.

Within weeks Emily's heart gave way and the staff commented, pausing at the empty little table, that perhaps she died of a broken heart. With no surviving family or friends, the staff were her only funereal mourners and Lyn was surprised when she was informed that Emily's will had stipulated that she receive the treasured locket. Lyn looked at the locket and a ditty she had learned as a child came into her head... a ditty that had always puzzled her, annoyed her almost. She took the locket home and placed it into a drawer where it lay eventually, apparently forgotten.

A year or so later Ben produced the locket and with it a sheet of paper.

'Interesting forensic results,' he dryly commented.

There were five examples of hair in the locket, from five different people, and all contained arsenic. Enough arsenic to kill. As Lyn's eyes widened in shock, then realisation the old ditty returned to her mind.

'A little man sat on a chair,
A little man who was not there,
He was not there again today –
O how I wish he'd go away.'

BOAT IN A BOTTLE

Anna was oblivious to the rolling wash of waves and the busy sea port noises behind her. Oblivious to the gulls squabbling in a swirl of shadows against the sun and of other sculptors working on huge granite blocks to make a line of art works on the ocean breakwater beyond Nobby's light.

Her bass relief design for the project was a 'Boat in a Bottle' and today she would begin.

Anna faced the two by three metre slab of grey granite. For luck, as always, she reached forward and touched the blank stone slab with her fingers.

A tingle raced up her arm.

An image like one seen out of the corner of her eye, and one she'd known for most of her fifty odd working years, was coupled in her mind with that tingle. The stone to mind contact always previously brought sculpting inspiration and success.

'Yes!' she breathed.

This sculpture was her retirement piece and she had, in preparation, driven to the southern coast shore to inspect the quarry site. Long Pacific swells smashed endlessly into huge granite pillars; some of which had broken away to fall in jumbled heaps below the cliffs. These stones had been retrieved and cut for the breakwater artists.

Anna grunted in effort as she lifted the spinning grinder blade to gouge in the background scene. The depiction of a horizon, a sky above with birds, clouds and a stormy sea emerged amid swirling stone dust. Far off a ship floundered. Finally, as her first work day was drawing to a close, she checked her cartoon and marked out the outline of the bottle. Her vision was of an ancient shape; squat and roundish with a long neck and a wide cork stopper. It would slant slightly from the horizontal as though it had washed up on an empty beach.

In the morning, she would start the delicate work to bring a young boy's slim figure, standing in a dingy racing before an approaching storm, out of the stone.

She was at her sculpture block at first light. The sun flickered out from its resting blanket of horizon clouds and touched the dozen bulk grain ships waiting for the pilot vessels to shepherd them into port. It lit her hands as she unerringly placed her chisel against the stone and tapped firmly with her hammer. Chips flew; the planes of a face and the rough-hewn hollows of eyes began to emerge.

'There you are,' she said to the image.

This was her magic moment. The thrill when she brought the subject of her sculpture out of the stone.

'Yes.' a gruff voice said. '...and you've taken long enough!'

She drew back, tools halted and looked around.

She was alone.

'Confound it woman! Don't stop! Keep going...' The voice was insistent. Commanding even.

A man's deep rumble came from the within the stone and quivered in the air around her.

'I don't know this place!' the voice said abruptly. 'Well, woman! Speak up!' A pause. 'I feel cramped. There's water over my ship... Where am I?'

'You're...' she hesitated. How could she tell him he didn't exist? 'What ship?' She asked the age-old standard sea enquiry.

'*The Astral*'. We left London, summer of 1878, bound for Sydney with a full cargo and passengers. Man overboard at the Cape of Good Hope...another night...terrible storm...we're on the rocks!' The voice shook. 'She broke up. I tried to launch the life boat but that floundered too. We're all drowned...I remember now.'

The voice petered out to silence.

It spurred the chisel in her experienced hands to cut boldly again into the grey stone. She flaked and detailed out the figure. The person emerging wasn't that of the gracile boy she had planned, but instead that of a robust man. She shaped tufts of hair curling on a broad brow under a seaman's cap, a woollen jersey open at the neck and sleeves rolled up to the forearms, all with sure strokes.

Anna eased the facial features out of the granite just as she sensed they were there; furrowed brows above deep eyes and lips pulled back in concentration. A clenched jaw. It was a strong handsome face, and in that instant she felt a surge of compassion for this lost soul she was somehow drawing from the rock.

Instead of the child's dingy she'd originally drawn she enlarged the craft to a ship's life-boat now with a mast. A sailor's firm hand held the tiller under a triangular shadow of sail. Wild broken seas and rocks on a headland – all depicted within the bottle-shape. She worked possessed with the urge to release the scene. But she shied away from more work on the face. She wasn't ready for the interaction with this figure, this man, again although her whole being wanted to know more.

She needed to know about her long memory of this man.

The image and face that had waited for her over the years. The man she knew now to be a sailor.

Inevitably she was compelled to work on the final sanding of his face and figure. Immediately again she felt a stirring of the being within.

'I'm dead, aren't I?' The wistful voice held regret.

'I don't know...but I think you are.'

Anna wanted to speak gently but she had to shout against the roar of a huge ship's engine, the pounding propeller, as a vessel approached the breakwater to dock in the port. She shrugged off an embarrassment as the artist working next to her looked at her oddly when she yelled at the stone face. He could be ignored – but the face and voice couldn't.

'What's that?' the voice demanded. 'It's a great ship!' It was almost as if the face was looking at the world past her shoulder. 'By Jove! It's one of those new ones. Metal and powered. It's got no sails! It's amazing!'

She moved aside as if to let the figure see the incoming vessel and the horizon with the convoy of waiting ships. The seaman's eye sockets caught a slant of sunshine and glowed with light. 'Yes, it is.' was all she could say.

'Are they cargo ships? What's the cargo? Do they have passengers?' The questions tumbled out in a torrent.

'They're bulk coal carriers and no, they don't carry passengers,' Anna said.

'Where will they go with their cargo? To England?'

The thrashing lessened as the ship passed. An attending tug hooted.

'They're destination is usually the Middle East, China and Asia.' She didn't have to shout any more.

'Set me free,' the voice suddenly demanded. 'I can join that ship...wherever it's going.'

'You can't ...' There was no explanation that Anna could give but she felt instinctively that he had to remain. Truth was her only option. 'You're stone. My carving's let you out... but you have to stay here.'

'No! I must go! You can't keep me.'

'I'm sorry...so sorry,' she said.

In silence Anna completed the details of the glass bottle with the huge cork stopper that was an essential part of her design. So far, he apparently, wasn't aware that he and his boat were inside the glass bottle shape.

The grand opening was planned for the next day at the head of the breakwater. Despite the continual protests from deep inside the stone and the feeling that she was being watched by the lovingly carved eyes that followed her every move, Anna had finally completed the work. There was no doubt about the pull she felt for the figure, almost as though, as she fancifully thought, she had known him all her life.

A past life?

Maybe she'd been a passenger on *'The Astral'* and died with him. Perhaps their souls were linked? Fanciful. But maybe?

Boat in a Bottle. It was done – her last commission. Different from the surrounding sculptors' works of fish, whales and ships but it was as Anna meant it to be. Her contact; her sailor had a face and a home.

A final resting place.

Overnight there was a huge storm. The estuary breakwater was washed by massive seas that arched and crashed over the stones and sculptures. Strands of weed clung to the bases of all the works.

It was mid-morning. A crowd gathered and applauded as the Town Mayor declared the exhibits opened.

'It's a gorgeous piece...but why did you carve the bottle as broken?' a friend asked Anna.

'What? I didn't!'

She ran down the length of the breakwater.

It was almost as if someone had damaged the bottle. Had the stone been glass it would have been cracked in a line that extended from the cork to the base. She opened her mouth to protest that the storm had damaged her work when she saw that the figure's eyes no longer seemed to look at her, to follow her. They stared out to sea.

Empty hollows.

But there was the slightest hint of a curl in the mouth that she didn't remember carving.

Anna placed her hand against the face.

There was the residue of a tingle.

It passed and was gone...as did the faint smile of farewell.

Her sailor had returned to the sea.

THE GIFT

I don't usually talk to strangers. Especially the clean good-looking ones. They don't usually talk to me either. But this man looked OK. In these days of the twenty-second century not everyone did – look OK I mean. Most of us are dirty, thin and scraggy, old before our time because poor food, contaminated water supplies and over population strained every resource. It wasn't the best of times...

Anyway, this young good-looking man approached me. Bought me a food drink and smilingly he made the offer.

'Wow!' I said in tired disbelief. 'You'd give me $100,000 to transform my body.'

His smile didn't falter. He nodded. I rushed on.

'I'll be OK?'

He nodded again.

I laughed. 'OK I'm yours. Transform me!' He smiled and we headed back out into the street.

The Street – well hardly a street! Not in the City.

The overcrowded grey alleyways were filled with uncollected rubbish, all picked over by the street kids and the millions of zonked out druggies. Zonked out and placid on State supplied drug tablets. At least I wasn't one of them. I'd kept my body and clothing as clean as I could, given my weary thirty years as one of the disadvantaged. Only the elite, the space jockeys, the well-fed bureaucrats and the wealthy could live on real food instead of the State supplied Sustenance Biscuits. The privileged lived comfortably as ever. With no work and somehow keeping off the drugs, I spent as much time as possible in the old libraries. They were at least open and free. From my reading of history times hadn't changed much. I read of revolution and a few of us had started to talk a little about change and the old notions of equality. We met on a semi regular basis and the $100,000 would maybe be useful to the group...someday.

The man led me to what looked on the outside as just another tatty grey building. Inside was warm with a clean reception area. Soft and inviting sofas lined the walls and I sank into the depths of instant luxury. All was quiet, blissful after the cacophony of the screaming streets.

A beautiful young woman came towards me. She smiled. I almost looked around – people don't smile much at me any more. She placed an envelope in my hands and discretely turned away as, doubtful as ever, I counted the legal tender chips. 'Yep, $100,000.' I thought.

She'd bought a cotton hospital type gown and she motioned me towards a cubicle to change.

'Come this way. Bring your envelope, if you want,' she said and bestowed another smile. I followed her, clutching my prize.

I stepped into the small room. The door shut and I shed my street clothes and changed into the clean gown. Suddenly the world went white. Blinding, eye burning white as sterilisation beams shot through me. My skin seared away. It fell around my feet in flakes like dirty snow. It numbed my brain. The envelope dropped. I watched in those last seconds – eons of slow motion. The envelope and chips slid into a moving slot on the floor. Disappeared. I stood in mute realisation.

A voice, soothing as cool untainted water, beguiling even, washed over me.

'You will be transformed,' it said. There was music. 'Transformed to keep the status quo. Transformed so that others may live.'

I was past movement. I sank to the floor, slow like my thoughts. The realisation was strong. Even OK.

I was tomorrow's Sustenance Biscuit.

A TIME TO ESCAPE

This was the outback country he was familiar with. Twin hills arched away from the secret strip where a lone plane had delivered an illicit payload that evening. The air was night crisp, grabbing at his lungs with sharp nailed fingers. He coughed against the cold and risked a glance over his shoulder. The bastards were still coming down from the higher drop country.

Didn't they ever give up? Hardly! The price was too high.

They were firing blindly like the gun happy idiots they were. He sensed the passage of a bullet passing his shoulder before he heard the retort, and he somersaulted into the nubbly scrub beside the track. Wriggling down behind a fallen tree trunk, he decided that he was probably going done this time. Lose first. the consignment of ice in the back pack strapped to his back. More likely then lose his life or at least his kneecaps. Same outcome. He pulled the pack free and stabbed his knife into the first of the leather bags setting the drug spilling out like white diamonds, as the addicts often called it. After cutting the bags fore and aft, he swung them, scattering the contents. He almost laughed as he left the carnage behind and scuttled further into the bush. That would take a while for them to attempt to find and scoop up the drugs. Maybe he'd have a chance to flee as they scrabbled about in the red dust. Best case scenario was that they'd try to sample the merchandise and rot either by their own hands or when the boss found out their treachery. Their idiocy.

It had begun in the first dawn light when the escorting heavies had tried to jump him for the merchandise, he'd been consigned to provide out of the Middle East for the Christmas drug rush. He could handle one or two of the morons, but when all five tried to relieve him of the consignment, he knew he was outnumbered. He took off grabbing a handful of car keys, chucked them away as he ran, then picked wrong escape car himself. The bloody thing had run out of fuel after the first couple of kilometres. Now he was on foot and he could hear them roaring after him, swerving on the bush tracks. There was a crump of metal as their one of heavy utes smashed into his stalled car. He smiled, a good idea to leave it stranded across the track. Now most would be on foot and, even if this wasn't his usual country, he knew he was better than the city street gangs, out here in unfamiliar territory.

How in the hell had he agreed to this plot to beat the gangs who trafficked in ice and other delights in time for Christmas cheer on the underworld dark streets of the city. He knew he was done even if he survived. There went his career. His future. Shit. He'd end up clambering down ship's filthy holds searching out illegals, or on Darwin's wet streets looking for kids smoking pot, instead of chasing the big boys in their lush offices of Sydney, where a man could wear a designer suit and make use of his university degrees. He'd not signed up for this. He'd bet his boss, in Sydney, was wrapped around his blonde bird and a whiskey glass, this Christmas Eve.

Another rattle of bullets was fired into the night. Torches flashed in the dark skies. out into the desert and low bush. Morons, he thought. It didn't help him any but made him relish their frustration and desperation. Maybe he could survive the night, if none of them tripped over him. He could hear them yelling to each other and shouting threats at him. As if he'd answer?

As the night went on the voices calling threats got fainter. Probably the goons had found enough of the scattered drugs to get a night's comfort this festive eve. He chuckled as his phone pinged. 'Finally found you,' said the voice he hoped was headquarters triangulating his position from his phone. 'Will pick you up in ten. Merry Christmas.'

The incoming chopper blades sounded to him like Santa's sleigh bells...

THE WEDDING FLOWER

'You have to understand I was…just a kid at the time. I wasn't told the full story. Just that they were dead.' Lisa shook her head of grey curls then scratched at her scalp.

'What are you referring to?' I asked, stopping the scratching old hand.

The scratching had stopped and now her hands gripped together. 'You asked me why I'd changed my name by deed poll,' she said.

'That was months ago when we were first talking about the kid's wedding,' I said. 'You mentioned that you'd changed your name. I thought that I'd been Gertrude or some grandmotherly name before you'd become Lisa. So, what was it and why now?'

'Well,' the pause lengthened and the hair re-arranged again. 'Someone's writing a book about them and has put it in…their deaths I mean.'

'You've only said that your parents died in a car crash. In the bush wasn't it?'

'At Wanna actually…' Lisa teethed her bottom lip.

Curiosity was killing me but I could see that she was having trouble with whatever she wanted to explain. I didn't feel that I needed to explain but she was obviously rattled. What on earth could come out in a book which would alter anything. 'OK, then first what was your name before you changed it. Might make the story easier to tell.'

'Daisy Fairy Lights,' she mumbled.

I clamped my lips together against a chuckle. 'Daisy Fairy Lights?' I repeated. 'Lisa's certainly better…' I got out past my need to laugh. 'Go on. Tell me more.'

'You have to understand it was the sixties. Dad and Mum were right into it. Hippies with the music, probably drugs and things.' Lisa was leaving her hair alone now, but a button on her blouse was getting twisted hard.

I leaned forward and stopped her hands again. 'Look, we've been friends for ages, and our children are getting married in a month. How can this book change things?'

'It tells how they died.'

'That's sad,' I said, 'but I repeat, how can it change anything?'

Lisa blurted out 'The writer got the coroner's reports. It said that my parents were found at the base of the cliff still in their old car. It wasn't in gear and only the hand brake was on. My father probably knocked the brake and they rolled over the cliff.'

'That's sad. but I can't see why you are so upset. It's so long ago.'

'They were naked and in position still...' Lisa's words were a mumble.

'In position still?' I queried.

'The report said that they were hard at it. In flagrante delicto.' She was trying to be delicate. Carefully choosing her words in some embarrassment.

'Must have been some free fall,' I said on wonderment, before doing my lip clamp again.

Lisa's eyes glared at me. 'See! You think it's funny. How are we to have a family wedding with this rotten book coming out before it? We'll be the laughing stock.'

My voice was a hiccough as I suppressed laughter. 'Come on Lisa, we'll think of something.'

'Well...It's a good thing that my grandparents are dead. They brought me up very properly and things like this weren't spoken of.' A smile flickered on Lisa's lips. 'Bill knows of course, in fact he loves the story. Teases me...'

'And our Grace? Our Steve? The're soon to be married couple?'

'No.'

'Well, we'll just have to tell them before the book comes out and before the wedding.' I let a chuckle of mischief creep into my voice. 'Perhaps since everyone will know by then, we could make a feature of the wedding of it. We're in different times now from when your grandparents were so shocked. Maybe in Bill's speech he could call you Daisy Fairy Lights and refer to the family's history of 'Romantic ends'...'

Lisa caught the joke. 'Jan!' she said in mock reproach. 'Off the cliff in love...' she ventured.

'A wedding of naked rapture? No, maybe that's going too far.' I laughed.

'All we've got to do now is tell the bride and groom.' Lisa's eyes became wide and she caught her lip.

'Maybe they know something. Grace has chosen daisies as her theme...'

'So, all we've got to add in is naked angels!'

FIVE COPPER COINS

Sarah dropped an old tatty chocolate box onto the table.

'What's in this, Mum?' she asked.

It had begun when Sarah wanted more space for her things and the only place available was in a tall cupboard in the hall. Already bored with the process of clearing it, she had pulled the box down from the top shelf and was ready to discard it after the briefest of appraisals.

Sarah opened the cardboard box and shoved the contents around. 'It's only old photos. Postcards and stuff. They can all be thrown out,' she declared.

Her abrupt opinion made Maggie look up from her magazine. She waggled her fingers at her daughter. Sarah sighed in exaggerated exasperation and scratched at her itchy scalp under the bandanna scarf she wore. Glancing down into the box again as she passed it to her mother, she picked out a photograph.

'Hang on,' Sarah interrupted herself. 'Look at this one! It's me! Yuk! Pigtails!' She tossed the photograph disgustedly aside.

As the photo flipped onto the table Maggie was drawn back...

'Look at me, Mummy!'

An action photograph. Sarah caught in mid air. Six years old. Skipping rope. Thick dark hair in ribboned pigtails flying. A black and white photo taken with an old 35mm camera. Maggie remembered again the green ribbons and red skipping rope. Sarah laughing...

Maggie stared and then, seeing her daughter's impatient attitude, looked into the box.

'These are old,' she agreed.

Her glance rested briefly, worriedly, on her pale daughter before she leafed through the uneven pile of black and white photos. One caught her eye. It showed a group of women and children picnicking on a long wide beach.

'Look, this one has your grandmother in it,' she stopped. Thought a moment. 'No,' Maggie decided, 'this'd have to be your great grandmother.'

Sarah feigned an interest, peering over her mother's shoulder. By today's standards the group looked awful. Long bulky skirts, dark frumpy cardigans and ankle strap shoes.

'Call the paramedics!' the teenager joked. 'They're an emergency overdose of yuk!' She smiled at her own cool comment and looked again. 'Which one's her?'

Maggie pointed.

Sarah leaned closer. At least that one didn't look quite as bad as some of the others. The woman wore her hair drawn back, a white blouse and a floral skirt. The group's severe hairdos and lack of make-up was hardly becoming for any of them.

David, Sarah's younger brother, came to the table from the fridge where he had been foraging. He pulled a face at his sister then rummaged through the chocolate box. He found five Australian pennies and decimal coins. All copper coins. He flipped the pennies over to look at the dates.

'No 1930 penny! That'd have been worth something.' He shrugged. 'Pity…'

He lost interest and shuffled off to his room. They heard the click as his computer was turned on followed by the thudding bounce of a basketball while he waited for the disc drive to crank up. Maggie sighed. It was no use remonstrating about the noise. The bouncing stopped to be replaced by the howl of a computer game's raucous introduction.

Maggie mentally blanked out the noise.

School skirt flying Sarah kept skipping. Maggie felt as if she was moving around her daughter as though taking photographs from a merry-go-round. It was an odd giddying sensation.

Maggie picked up the photo of her grandmother again. She shook her head trying to concentrate. She felt the strain of these last months.

'This was taken here, in Port Lincoln,' she forced herself to continue. 'Your great grandmother came here to work as a governess.' She picked through the box again. 'Yes. Here's a postcard addressed to her mother.' She peered at the faded postmark. 'It's dated December 1939. About the time she met your great grandfather who was going off to the war.'

There was a small magnifying glass in the box and pretending curiosity Sarah looked closely at the photo. She scanned along the row of faces until her great grandmother's young face leapt into view. She looked up sharply.

'She looks like me!' she blurted.

Maggie chuckled at her reaction. 'You look like her, you mean.'

Sarah grunted, not sure if she should be pleased or dismayed. There went her teenage dream world. When her brother became too much of a nuisance or when her parents insisted, she was still too young for some things she could convince herself that she was adopted. So much for that fantasy of a rich family who would one day claim her.

She stopped herself.

That was before. At fourteen she needed a fantasy. Especially now...

She turned again to the copper coins.

'Hey, this two-cent coin's my birth year... and here's yours,' Sarah announced with an 'I know how old you are' smirk at Maggie. She turned the two coins over. Yes, there was the Queen on both of the reverses. The older three pennies had George V1, George V and Queen Victoria on the backs. The old Queen's face had the scowl she remembered from history lessons. 'What a grump,' Sarah stated as she held out the coins to her mother.

Maggie smiled. 'Yes, this one's my mother's birth year and the older ones must be my grandmother's and great grandmother's.'

'I can jump 100 hundred times,' the younger Sarah boasted. She started to count. '1...2...3...4...' Her feet tripped the rope and she started skipping again. '1...2...3...4...5...'

Sarah placed the coins on the table and, delving back into the box, she found more photographs. She scooped everything up into a little pile and abruptly turned back to the clearing job.

Maggie sighed. Feeling dismissed. Feeling inept.

She and Sarah had been so close. Before the sickness. Now Sarah refused to really talk about it. To express her fears. 'Denial,' the counsellors said. She needs a positive attitude to help the fight. To help the treatments.

Soon the chemotherapy should cleanse the leukaemia from her body in preparation for the T-cells from David. He was offhand about it but had offered to be tested and be the donor. Twelve years old and Internet proficient he'd looked it all up. He wasn't keen on the process of bone marrow garnering but even he had not been able to break through his sister's defences. She had accepted his offer with a shrug and changed the subject to questions about losing her hair.

Now her beautiful hair was gone.

Maggie's eyes threatened to spill over with tears.

Maggie spun around her daughter as she jumped. Sarah in black and white with the red rope and green hair ribbons blurring with movement. She held her breath as she watched her skip. For no reason she could explain this was important. '...55...56...57...' Sarah counted as her feet flew over the rope. She had got this far...

'Mum?' Sarah's voice cut into the whirl of her thoughts. 'Can I have these?'

Maggie blinked back to the moment as Sarah picked up the photographs and coins. She looked blankly at her.

'I'd like to have these framed. They'd look good in my room.' Sarah's comment and request were quiet.

Intense.

Instinctively Maggie treated it casually. 'Of course, we can have them framed tomorrow.'

In the morning her father took Sarah into town and handed over his credit card. She insisted on taking the coins and photos into the picture framers on her own.

The rope swung crookedly. Sarah faltered then regained her balance. '...96...97...98...'

A week later a large frame lay on the table wrapped in white tissue paper. Covered. Hidden.

Maggie waited.

Sarah made herself a large mocha-chocolate milkshake and sat perched sideways on a chair beside it. She took a sip of her drink.

'You can have a look,' she said, intuitively aware that her mother's need to see inside the parcel was more than curiosity.

Maggie pulled the gilded framed picture free of the paper. Set into an expensive cream satin background the matriarchal photographs and copper coins were lined up chronologically and marched down the picture frame from the oldest to the present day. At Sarah's position was her coin, her baby photograph and, Maggie felt her throat tighten, beside it the black and white skipping photograph.

The hair ribbons had been hand tinted green and the rope coloured red.

Maggie opened her mouth to ask. Why? How?

Sarah pointed to empty spaces lower in the frame.

'I don't know where I will get a copper coin for my baby when I'm old enough to have one, she said. 'There's no more two-cent pieces being made.' Her gaze was open and smiling at her mother. 'Do you think a gold dollar will be all right?'

'...99...100. See I can do it, Mum!'

DIRTY WASHING

When he switched on the light he saw...the huge pile of ironing waiting. This wasn't unusual but it was 3 am and his telephone pager had just gone off.

Where to find a wearable shirt and get to the hospital? Life used to be easy when Liz was still with him. Washing and ironing done, meals and everything else. The everything else was probably the best...he smiled to himself. And she worked shifts as an agency nurse at the hospital. Still, he thought, his smile vanishing into the muddle of clothing in the basket, she wasn't called back at all hours of the sodding night to attend to patients. Probably something trivial, or not, he cautioned himself to hurry up. She was probably still tucked up in her bed asleep. Somewhere. Not in his bed. When they were together, she would have opened one eye at least to acknowledge that he was going.

'Shit! He spat the oath aloud. This wasn't even clean clothing. He hadn't done the washing in ages. He stormed past the kitchen with its dishes in the sink, take-away pizza boxes mainly. Got to find a shirt somewhere. The wardrobe. He grabbed the first one that his hand hit.

Even if he was slack at home, he did think that the patients deserved a clean shirt, not a T shirt, whenever he attended them. Gave them confidence...and he felt better too. He thrust his legs into his black trousers and small change and his car keys spilt out onto the floor. He scrabbled for the keys and found one shoe. 'Where the hell is the other one!' he stormed, aware that he was taking too much time to get to the hospital. Found it and out the door. In the car he calmed down.

It wasn't Liz's fault that things had got into the muddle. I'm a selfish bastard! He remonstrated as he just caught the lights near the hospital. Will have to get my act together. Send Liz some flowers, anything, promise her the earth and try to keep the promises. She's the one…

He pulled into the doctor's parking bay and sped into the hospital, into the lift and arrived puffing at the Nurses station.

Liz looked him up and down.

'Mr Baker isn't so good,' she said. 'His pain's worse and his blood pressure has been falling over the last hour.' She handed him Mr Baker's charts, all professional. He took the charts, his mind already working on the patient. He looked at Liz; she looked so beautiful, so good.

Liz led the way to the patient's room and handed him a sterile gown to put over his clothes. 'Better have this,' she said dryly. 'Wouldn't want to ruin your good dinner shirt. You've obviously been out on the town…'

IF IT AIN'T BROKE...!

The computer margins moved again and my words and sentences rearranged themselves in erratic strips across the screen.

'Botheration!' I grunted.

I flicked the pointer arrow at a decal and it all returned to normal. I really had to do something about that annoying margin problem. Try to fix it. Something told me to turn the power off at the switch: you do that with toasters, I reckoned in my computer ignorance. The battery should be enough, but I didn't do it.

Instead, I moused into 'Properties' until the screen was layered. Layer upon layer like a Sarah Lee cake concoction.

'One more should fix it,' I thought before my mind wandered off thinking about the images of the layers like cloud banks heralding a storm or a deck of cards strewn across a table... I do that being somewhat of a poet.

Suddenly the screen flashed white! Everything on it was gone! I cussed again as Matrix like, the new-fangled mouse I'd been given at Christmas bucked in my hands. With a whoosh it sucked me up the cord and into the machine. Flattening and stretching my ample figure I tried to scramble back along the heaving and bucking cord to the outside. I was squeezed; it took some doing I can tell you, through pillars of zeros and ones – millions, zillions of them. Zeros pushed down onto my head. They squashed my shoulders and the ones poked into my nose and eyes. They plunged between my toes and threaded and combed themselves into my hair like cosmic hair extensions. Then my body was suddenly elongated so that its' width was thinned to individual molecules. Atoms to DNA level.

Hope began to fade as my individual brain molecules stretched to ones and zeroes…

I screamed but no noise came through the vacuum of computer space. The margin control came within recognition and reach and I grabbed at it. It slunk away whipping and bending in margin merriment. Margin glee! I could sense my millions of typed words, the poetry, the stories, the film script and novels jumping back and forth trying to gain the own freedom and recognition as the manic mouse came back. The words dissolved into ones and zeros, and I shied away screaming again as they melded back into me. Back to their origins.

It was no use…

I'm still in the computer.

The complete disappearance of a lone lady writer had the police and authorities mystified. They wound up my estate and sold my old dinosaur computer by the kilogram as trash. I'm now with it dumped on an artificial reef with old cars and washing machines to attract fish. The water has seeped in and I watch the fish peering into my screen. They are really quite good company as they go about their colourful lives.

But I should have left well alone…

It hadn't been broken…

THE DANCING LADY

Lola pointed a fluffy slippered foot at the wood heap, bowed with a sweeping gesture enhanced by a yellow feather duster, and danced sideways into the vegetable garden.

'*Her name was Lola, she was a showgirl...*' wafted clearly over the fence. '*With yellow feathers in her hair and a dress cut down to there...*' followed.

Sparrows fled on whirring wings as Lola lurched through tomatoes that Ted, her husband, had staked in their immaculate garden. Her wobbling pirouette carried her on through the pumpkin and sweetcorn patches.

I stared at my elderly friend through the gauze curtains of my window. She wore a long pink floral nightdress, a purple cardigan buttoned crookedly and a striped tea towel turban-tied through which her grey hair stuck out every which way.

The staid, the caring, the strong Lola?

Out of the garden beds she went. Arms swaying in total disregard to the direction of her dancing feet, she weaved across the lawn and sat down abruptly on a green garden seat.

'*Her name was Lola,*' she sang again and the feather duster conducted an unseen dance band.

It was six am and raining.

Raining hard – as it can in Spring.

I'm not usually up and about at that hour, being definitely an owl person. Most teenagers are and, although I wasn't an ordinary teenager any more, I still clung to teen ways. Encouraged by Lola I must add. I'd also been away for a couple of months so I was unaware of Lola's recent morning behaviour.

This couldn't be usual.

As she continued to sway to her own tune I hesitated. What should I do? Call out? Where was Ted?

The rain mellowed to a drizzle. Her tabby cat sauntered down the path towards her. It sheltered under her seat in the way of cats and licked raindrops from its fur. Abruptly Lola stood, gathered her sodden gown around her, and trailing the cat, danced up the path and through the back door into the house.

Problem solved for the moment.

I sat back and began my morning medication rituals. My head whirled. Lola acting in this amazing way and my drugs did that. Laughter bubbled. It shouldn't have but the absurdity of Lola dancing in the rain couldn't find a processing area in my brain.

No way! Not Lola!

I'd better go back to a beginning.

Ted and Lola have been our neighbours since forever, well since Mom and I moved here years ago after the bust up with Dad. Life was tough at first but it got better. My parents stopped quarrelling enough to communicate civilly when Dad arrived for access visits, and Ted and Lola decided that we weren't too bad. For a single parent family. They were much older than Mom, already grey haired, and had no children. Mom worked part time anyway and we did the right things like no loud music and we kept the garden neat. Well, Mom did the gardening and my loud music was sometimes a minor issue. Don't get me wrong we were not close neighbours, just saying 'hello' and Ted would pass delicious, home–grown tomatoes over the fence in Summer.

They were always Mr and Mrs Webb to me. It was that sort of relationship.

Things changed when I got sick.

I'm not going to go into the details of adolescent cancer, just that it hit us hard. Dad was working overseas and there wasn't other family support.

The Webbs stepped into the breach as if they had always been there. They didn't intrude but they helped. Helped Mom especially. At first, I was oblivious of them through the haze of shock, treatments, feeling ratshit, and teenage self-centred rebellion. This attitude finally drove most of my friends away and Mom shouldered me as she always had.

They, Ted and Lola, as Mom now called them, were just there, always there and I began to resent them for taking up my mother's time. My time. In petty juvenile retaliation I sang, loudly, renditions of 'Copacabana' out of my bedroom window overlooking their back yard.

Remember I was a very young, lost, a difficult and scared teenage patient then.

No excuse, I guess.

When Mom was working Lola started bringing books to help me fill in the time when I just lay about sick and miserable. She played on my name with the first book. 'Tess of the d'Ubervilles' a story of how that Tess had suffered hardships. Lola's way of encouragement!

I read Thomas Hardy, grudgingly; hating Tess's whining voice but the romantic, poetic and atmospheric words got through. I started reading, devouring books. With books I could disappear into different worlds, other worlds where there wasn't me – or pain. Books about people who knew who they were in their lives. I discovered that Lola had been an English teacher and she'd always been blighted by her name. Unwittingly, perhaps more teen contrary like, I'd revisited Lola's discomfort with my singing. As we became firmer friends, I apologised. She'd laughed and hugged me.

There was one small note of discord in the neighbourly relationship.

Dear old-fashioned Ted did not think that, a child – me – should have been told about the severity of my illness. I overheard them arguing once...

The rain started again and the broken plants proved what I had seen had really happened. I didn't know what to do, especially later, when Ted and Lola visited to welcome us home. I'd sent them a card from the city hospital, snail mail as they don't have e-mail, telling them that I was finally in remission and the doctors were optimistic. They were as normal as I had ever seen them; bringing another book for me and delight written all over their faces. I watched them warily – not trusting myself to say anything especially after I'd blurted out, 'I saw you Lola...dancing...this morning...'

Lola just smiled, looking as if I she hadn't heard or I hadn't said anything.

Ted's smile was slightly different. He glanced at Lola first. Did he know that she had danced like that? His slight frown to me said he did. He had to, given the trampled vegetable garden.

Mom's frown was different. It said 'Shut up!' I did and we got back to talking about our return home.

So, the weeks went on.

Many mornings I watched Lola dance in the back garden in her nightie and dressing gown. She often wore bright things, flowers or cloths, as hats. "*Lola was a showgirl...*" was the only song but I never heard her sing past those first words. She'd just trill '*La la la la...*'

After Lola danced Ted repaired the garden and they often visited, as before, in the afternoons. Sometimes we'd go shopping to buy a new scarf to hide my still naked scalp. My re-emerging hair worried Lola and she was most insistent that 'as a young lady you have dignity.' Other times we'd go for coffee or to the library for books. We'd laugh a lot but always about life and things happening around us.

Never about the dancing lady.

Lola was not quite the same. She couldn't remember where

she'd left things, or find the car in the parking lot by herself, and, long retired, she was often concerned that she'd be late for a school class and she hadn't marked homework. Ted would reassure her that it was holiday time. She was happy then, like when she was dancing.

But she'd look through me sometimes. Right through me. As if she didn't know me.

'Tess,' she'd say when she heard my name. 'Tess of the d'Ubervilles. That's Thomas Hardy's best book. Have you read it?'

A concerned look from Ted. He would never tell Lola anything that he felt would worry her.

Not about her health. Not that she was slipping away to a different place.

'I'll read it tonight,' I'd say, feeling silly repeating myself.

Lola would laugh. 'You'll never read it in one night,' she'd insist.

There was this thing happening. Lola helped me through my transition to acceptance that I might go where she is going now. Fight – but be prepared; almost like a Girl Guide creed. My reawakening that I would live was almost as hard for me. My old friends were doing different things. They'd moved on.

It's hard to reinvent yourself. To pick up the pieces of your life; and I almost have with study and meeting new people at uni.

But then – without a word from anyone about Lola – I knew what I wanted to do.

This morning, when Lola came into her garden, I climbed the fence and joined her. We danced separately, each to our own music. When Lola finished dancing, the cat appeared as always, and without a glance at me, they went silently indoors together.

It's my turn now – to be there for my dancing lady.

FLOWERS FOR RUTHY

'I couldn't believe it this morning! You won't believe it either!' Janet barely paused for breath. 'This morning, on my doorstep there was this man, all dossed up in fancy gear, with the biggest box in his hands, banging on the door, he was. 'Flowers', he says when I opened the door, flowers for our Ruthy. 'Put them somewhere cool,' he says, as if I didn't know what to do with flowers. He waited a bit, probably for a tip, but I closed the door in his smirking face. Sent him packing.'

'It was a huge box, very pretty from one of those fancy Mayfair florists – but sort of like a flat wide coffin,' Janet's eyes widened as she leaned on the back fence of the row of attached houses. 'Gave me a bit of a turn if I didn't know it was full of flowers.' Her neighbour nodded and tucked a scrap of hair back into her headscarf as she settled herself for what would be a long session.

'Who could be sending flowers to Ruthy?' she offered.

'The box was all closed up with tape but there was a tiny corner that came apart when I moved the box onto the kitchen table. Caught on the bread knife.' The other woman nodded again in agreement. Of course, there would be a way for a mother to check on these things. 'I could see roses, red and pink roses. Dozens of them with ribbons. Beauties too, and expensive. Very expensive. The colours were beautiful and they smelled lovely...' Janet's face softened as for an instant she allowed a small memory to impose into the dreariness of her life. She started, 'They needed water so I opened the box. Couldn't let them wither, could I?' Again, the nod of agreement from her listener.

'Was there anything else in the box?' she asked.

'There was a card hidden in the ribbons. 'Thank you for a wonderful night, Steve', it said.' Janet paused and the frowning response wasn't long coming.

'Isn't Ruthy walking out with Bob? Almost engaged you said. Who's this Steve?'

'Well maybe she's seeing someone new now. From the flowers he must be rich.'

The neighbour sniffed: her pending disapproval seeped out from under her scarf.

'Bit suggestive message,' she admonished.

'Ruthy's working for very important people. She works late for them. Nothing out of the ordinary for a girl who's been to typing school. Going up in the world is our Ruthy.'

'Well...' the neighbour conceded. 'My Frannie never got flowers like that.' Her parting shot brought bile up into Janet's mouth and she clamped her mouth shut and swirled the bitterness.

Suddenly Janet had work to do. She went back inside and furiously vacuumed the front room, then tidied the bedrooms. Especially Ruthy's room with all the recently acquired new clothes then prepared the evening family meal of sausages and chips. She waited, a fresh apron and a cup of tea at the ready to fortify herself.

The front door rattled and a smiling Ruth came in and dropped her keys on the kitchen dresser.

'Hi'ya Mum...' Ruth smiled.

'What have you been up to my girl...?' her mother demanded.

THE LAST PIE

'I've been a chef for twenty years or so. You've seen me on TV surely? No? Oh well, Your honour, please believe me, I didn't kill the entire film crew. Yes, I know – it was my last show, they'd cancelled me, and the crew was rude and less then enthusiastic when I was not satisfied with the pastry for my last pie. I'm a professional and naturally I insisted on preparing a new one. It did take a further hour and they were peeved at me. Stupid inferior youths! The director looked as though he was in his teens, for goodness sake, and impudent with it. Called me an old fart, Your Honour. I even had to bring in my own pots and chopping board to the last show because they had broken up my set. Can you imagine it? The humiliation of it!

My piecrust on the second attempt was perfect. I'd chopped chicken, herbs, truffles, bacon, etc, lovely ingredients. You must be a cook too, Your Honour, going by your ample girth under those robes, so you will appreciate the quality I describe. The final pie was wonderful, as you can imagine. The crew, as usual, ate it as soon as they had finished filming it. Ate it even as I was saying my final goodbye to my faithful audience. There was nothing in it that could cause harm, but they all took sick and were whisked away to hospital. Dead within the day so the police told me.

I wonder if there was a gas leak somewhere…? I'm sure I could smell gas…

You have to believe me, I'm not a mass murderer! The forensic people insisted that it was mushroom poisoning that killed the crew, and yes, I cooked mushrooms for my wife the night before. She ate her dinner and left me for my personal assistant when she found out that I had lost my TV show. I haven't seen either of them since… are they still missing?

Do I eat mushrooms, Your Honour? No! I don't eat mushrooms, Sir, loathe them. But it would be beneath my dignity to make a poison pie. I'm a professional…and I cannot understand what all the fuss is about…nothing to do with me…'

CATCHING SPARROW'S TAIL

Fear elbowed aside the flowing benefits of T'ai Chi. Tania breathed deeply and forced her concentration back.

Catching Sparrow's tail right
Catching Sparrow's tail left
Scoop up the sand, let go, push
Single whip

The rhythmic breathing helped as she turned with the exercise. Her father's grip lessened, for the moment.

White crane
Brush knee left, brush knee right
Swing punch, forward parry and punch

Tania could not understand the absurdity of her father allowing her to take T'ai Chi lessons each week when she was a virtual prisoner in his household. It was his quirk, perhaps to keep her guessing and off guard. Stop her if he thought she was enjoying them. Always holding her in his power like the dozens of phone calls that he made to her each day. To know what she was doing every moment.

At twenty years of age she was doing only what he allowed.

Not able to think, not able to act, not able to escape. Not like her mother who had fled the marriage all those years ago. He screamed that she was not going to 'abandon me – not like she did!' His obscenities were horrible against her mother, a mother Tania could not remember. Words that often became fists.

Flying hands
Catching hands
Needle on the seabed

Waving hands in cloud

She pretended indifference to the outing when the T'ai Chi movements, even the names of them, kept her sanity intact. He insisted she attended each week and sat in the car outside the hall where it was held. Sat there and talked into his mobile phone. Keeping the appearance that she was free and their lives normal. He attended the first few lessons with her. All charm to the other class members of course. Then he grew bored with it, ridiculed it but he allowed her to continue. He delivered her at the dot of five and expected her out the door precisely at six. No variations or there would be trouble.

She had attended school until the legal age of leaving when he had insisted, as he always did, that she had to look after the house and him. It was always that way. No school visits, no one allowed to come to the house. Friends were discouraged and they gave up. All except one. She met him when her father decided that she had to earn her keep, 'out in the real world'. He found her a job, part time, in a flower shop owned by a business acquaintance. Her pay was paid into his account but at least she was out of the house for a few hours a week.

There she met Darren when he came in one day when her boss was out. He made her smile. Tonight, something was going to happen.

Right kick, Left kick

Striking Tiger

Not that Darren would act alone. Her father was hated by many of his 'business acquaintances' she knew that. She had overheard phone calls. Calls when he had screamed threats down the phone. Mysterious strangers came to the house and she had recently discovered a locked safe that she had not previously known existed. One time a police officer had called at the house on a general inquiry and her father had questioned her for days and she had to repeat the simple conversation to him time and time again. Even then he was not satisfied.

Creeping Snake

Golden cock

Flying hand

Catching hand

Darren had given her a small parcel. 'Put it behind your father's car seat,' he'd said. And she had. She didn't want to know what it was. Couldn't think about it. Then she thought about nothing else as she had gone about her chores, exact household chores so that the house was perfect. Perfect father and daughter. Her movements faltered.

Elbow strike

Turn and Snake strike, swing punch

Retreat climbing over Tiger

The blast of the outside explosion blew in the windows and sent glass skidded across the parquetry floor. Class members screamed and instinctively fell back. Tania stayed stunned, silent. The hubbub of voices grew around her as people recovered and rushed to the window to look. She knew what had happened. The parcel had to be a bomb. A bomb she had placed. A bomb for her father.

Within minutes the police burst through the door. Guns drawn.

Darren, in police flak jacket, appeared. She could only stare at him. As her knees gave, he caught her and carried her into a side room. She was chanting the names of T'ai Chi movements. Words tumbled over each other. He shook her gently. Engulfed her. Kissed her face.

'I killed him! I killed him!' she babbled. 'The parcel...'

'No!' he insisted. 'No! I gave you a recorder. A voice recorder. You're free! Someone else wanted him dead much more than you did. It's over.'

Her bitter laugh was sobbing and hysterical. 'More than I did...that's not possible.'

The T'ai Chi leader came into the room. At a nod from Darren, she put her arm about Tania's shoulder. 'We all have to stay for police questions,' she said with a gentle smile. 'But we must calm down. Regain our Chi. Come.' She led Tania back into the main room. As the group slowly formed into their places Tania numbly complied.

Starting T'ai Chi

Catching Sparrow's tail right

She took a deep breath. She was free. No one would catch her tail again. She laughed. Her movements flowed...

Catching Sparrow's tail left

CITY IN A GLASS BLOCK

Paris... Romantic Paris. City of love. City of dreams.

City in a glass block.

City of curses...

The glass block arrived last week. Post marked 'Paris' and exquisitely packed. No distinguishable return address.

It was small; a tourist trinket, two and a half by five centimetres, the edges honed to smooth triangular shapes. Inside the clear glass were three etched images: the Arc de Triumph, the Eiffel Tower and Notre Dame. The ones you would expect, although the Eiffel Tower seems to have swirling fireworks depicted around its mast.

I held the glass in my hand. It was cold initially but it slowly warmed to my blood temperature.

'I love Paris in the spring time, when it sizzles. I love Paris in the fall, when it drizzles. I love Paris every moment...' rushed into my mind, like it had all those years ago. When Paris meant a city of dreams. People dream of Paris and I was no different.

It was September 1997, two weeks after Princess Diana had been killed in the Paris tunnel, when we arrived on our long planned and pre-booked European tour. My teacher friends and I had seen the despair in Britain, walked through what was left of the decaying flowers, and had been almost glad to leave London. London was not in a holiday mood.

European bus tours are for the fit. We were that, but the eternal bickering of some of the other tourists, and the very, very early morning starts through Germany, Switzerland and Italy was starting to get a bit much. We weren't young, fifties, and the prospect of Paris and a few days free time was looking like a good thing.

I also was to meet up with an old school friend who I hadn't seen in forty years. A few hours to reminisce. Although we'd never been close friends, Peter had been a bit of a nerd – a nice nerd – top of the class nerd and all that sort of thing, he and I had shared quite a few lunch hour conversations about books mainly. He liked Sci-Fi too; a secret we shared.

For some reason I'd been spooked since Rome with a feeling that something was wrong. To make things worse I felt that it was here in Europe, not family at home in Australia. I'm usually right about these odd feelings...

We arrived at the Paris hotel entrance, after the slow chaos of Paris traffic and an unavoidable run through 'that' tunnel. It was raining. For the first time on the tour it was raining, cold miserable autumn rain. Paris streets and spires seemed to shine through it but the people looked harried. Elegantly bedraggled. We got out of the bus and were immediately drenched.

Suddenly out of nowhere this gypsy woman stood beside me. She was young, her belly was swollen with child, breasts heavy and a toddler clung to her skirts. She held her hand out to me obviously begging. As I fumbled with my purse and bags the bus driver hurried over to us and shouted at her. He was yelling at her in the rain. I wanted to give her something but I had no franks, no negotiable money. This was before the Euro when, in each country, we struggled with finances.

The woman shied away but instead of cursing the bus driver she turned black angry eyes on me. Curses in French tumbled out of her mouth. They felt like curses. They had to be curses because the driver went white, and screamed again at her.

Suddenly she stood stock still and pointed a wet dripping hand into my face.

'You!' she screamed in English. She ran a cold finger down my cheek. The mark stung. I pulled away. 'You!' she said again. 'You! I know you! You are cursed. You will be cursed in Paris. You can never be happy in Paris!'

The driver and a security guard shooed her away and the flow of our bus load of people moved me inside the foyer. The bus driver returned. 'It's nothing,' he quickly assured me. 'Nothing.' He appeared to force a smile. 'Gypsies don't like red haired people.'

I was not so sure. From that moment bad things started. Not to me but to others around me. My friends. That night Jan lost her purse and all her documents. Ray and Louise got bad news from home and made plans to leave the group in the morning, and the tour guide was less than useful in it all.

CAT

Our old cat died last week.

At 17 plus she had run her race and simply faded away. There is no question of ownership, although we called her ours, and in the way of the best of cats we didn't own her – we belonged to her.

Puss was a beautiful creature, a longhaired tabby with exquisite markings and large splashes of white. She could hold her place in any beauty ranks and well she knew it. As with all our previous cats she came unannounced. Given to us with a gruff, 'Found her on my place. Was going to shoot her as a stray, then thought you were soft enough to give her a home. She was already just past the kitten stage and had been desexed – still had the blue stitches in her side. We did the usual; contacted the vets and put an ad in the paper. No one knew her or claimed her and after a hassle when I removed the sutures, she moved in.

Family life was never the same. The boys, rowdy and clumsy preteens, became enlisted as her willing allies. House rules were demolished as she commanded sleeping spots on the ends of beds, sunny areas wherever she chose and was always in the way. She was adept at pretending it was too cold to be put out at night and stayed by the fire with her 'poor cat look' and a very satisfied purr. Puss draped over chairs and windowsills contemplating universal questions, or sleeping – it was hard to tell the difference. She never explained her actions as no aristocratic cat ever does.

She plonked herself into the middle of any game or paper spread on the floor, rearranged war games pieces, chessmen, knitting and pencils. Puss kept her contract as a mouse-catcher par excellence but twice she brought live mice into the house to present to us, then dropped them. Result – we were the ones chasing mice for days!

She was belled for chasing birds.

Usually, with us, her manners were perfection itself with conversational 'please' and 'thank-you' in mews and purrs. She could admonish when she felt it necessary. Once she gently bit a friend of the boys, who had, obviously in her opinion, behaved with less than gentlemanly manner with her. They remained friends and he was most contrite. With us, if we displeased her, like coming home from an obvious fishing trip with no fish for her, or any other misdemeanour, she would give us 'the back'. Sometimes, in cat fashion we would get 'the back' just because she needed, at that moment, to reaffirm that she was a cat and not a fawning dog, thank you!

With other animals Puss was not a lady and her manners lacked a certain classiness. Other cats, – except an elderly one–eyed neighbour cat with whom she would share sleeping spots on the roof on lazy autumn mornings – and dogs were dispatched out of the yard in a fury. If the offending animal were not speedy enough it would be put right out of the street. Puss would return, hissing dark comments about the trespasser and demand to go onto the balcony where she could oversee her domain again. Grooming was meticulous on those occasions.

When Puss was 15 years of age, we moved house to a five-acre lot with a very extended horizon. She was now quite deaf and slow and we worried about her ability to adjust. What a laugh! After days of spookiness, when she scuttled from furniture to door to deck, she found her comfort zone and conquered the new property. A pert youthfulness was regained and she oversighted the work to be done, sitting with dignity just where rocks were to be moved, perched on the completed fish pond walls, she attended barbecues, and demanded her usual attention from us and any guests. The birds soon learned that she was harmless and teased her. We never witnessed how she coped initially with the electric fence that kept the cattle steers in the paddock but she always lowered her tail when she went under the wires. Whenever we went out, she followed, calling and conversing loudly – a noisy demanding shadow.

Last weekend Puss attended her last function; and then when all the family had sat with her, stroked and petted her, and said 'Goodbye' she was gone. She now has a secluded final place, with a view, and the morning sun. A new tree has been planted near to commemorate her life and give her shelter when the days become hot or too cold.

Puss was present at most of the rights of passage for us all during her long life. We played together, laughed with and at her, celebrated graduations together, and we cried tears into her fur in the bad times. She was there to gently stroke when we were reflective or stressed. Of course we loved her, in fact were quite dotty about her. Will we be crass enough to want another cat after her? Naturally – yes we will. The relationship was so good that we will be delighted, in time, when another cat chooses us, elicits our love, and rearranges our lives to suit herself.

Next time we may even agree on a name...

THE TIN TRUNK

Miss Thomas sat fidgeting, which was not her usual manner, before the dusty tin trunk that sat ingloriously on a thick bundle of newspapers on her mahogany dining room table. It had been there since the day before when an electrician, repairing old wiring inside the ceiling, had called out to her as she was sipping her morning tea.

'Found this, love. What do you want me to do with it?'

He'd smiled and she was too surprised, shocked even, to more than hurry to get the newspapers to protect her parents' table. He had heaved it downstairs with great ease and thumped it down on the protective papers. Now, as the doorbell rang heralding the daily visit of her neighbour, she shrugged towards the trunk still unsure of what to do next.

'Hello Miss Thomas,' Jacqui, her neighbour's the fourteen-year-old daughter, called. 'Mum's got another appointment. I'm here today to help you.' The slim, denim skirted girl came in through the back door, pecked her on the cheek with a familiar kiss and grinned, 'How are you today?'

Although Miss Thomas was nearing ninety years old, she and Jacqui were friends. Miss Thomas had lived alone next door all Jacqui's life and the cross-generation bond was strong. Now the child's eyes lit up with curiosity at the sight of the trunk. 'What's that? she asked.

'It's my old school trunk.' Miss Thomas said softly. 'I thought that my parents had thrown this away sixty years ago.' The softness became a sigh. She looked at Jacqui well aware that the moment had come. 'Will you help me open it now?'

Within moments the key, still tied to the trunk's handle by a leather string, turned in the scratchy lock and Jacqui carefully opened the lid. After a nod from Miss Thomas, she lifted back a linen cloth cover and revealed a whiteness below. On top was a long pair of gossamer gloves, lacy spider web soft and fragile. She placed them close to Miss Thomas and reached in again.

The old lady stroked them and her eyes seem to glaze as her thoughts fled back from the room and into the past. Jacqui slowly lifted a white satin and lace ball gown from under the linen cloth. Tiny gossamer white feathers were woven into the neckline and taken down the back into a long elegant train. The gown was carefully folded but as she shook it gently and held it before her it flowed down from her hands into its natural folds, as though the gown was just waiting to be free again.

'It's lovely! Gorgeous!' Jacqui breathed. 'I've never seen feathers on a dress before.' She gently touched the train. 'So soft. I can't believe how soft these are.'

Miss Thomas smiled brought back willingly by the child's words.

'It's my debutant dress.' She offered. 'I wore it when I was presented to the King and Queen at Court.'

Jacqui's face registered confusion and Miss Thomas smiled again.

'In my day most girls 'Came Out' and were presented in society to show they were ready for marriage. Some of us even went to London from Australia for the whole debutant season.' She continued, her eyes alight, although she was aware that Jacqui still didn't really understand. 'Oh, we had a wonderful time, the balls and the grand house parties, even fox hunting. Two of my friends married into the aristocracy, as my parents wanted me to' she confided. 'But I didn't find anyone to love, not there.'

The old lady lifted more tissue paper from inside the trunk.

'And here's my fur stole.' She said. It was again white and the fur still was soft and resilient. A faint hint of lavender eased out of the folds as she held it to her face.

'People don't wear fur these days,' Jacqui said with a firm resolve. 'It's not considered proper or kind to the animals to kill them for their fur.'

'Yes, I know,' said Miss Thomas. 'But things were different then. Maybe it isn't right now.' She stroked the fur and the faraway look returned. 'I only wore this for that one season in London,' she said.

Miss Thomas gathered sepia photographs from the bottom of the trunk. 'See,' she said and layed them out. As Jacqui held the gown against herself the old lady said. 'I wanted this to be my wedding dress but...' She looked down and shuffled the photos together to hide her tearing eyes as the memories crowded. 'Another young man at home, was unsuitable, as he was just the son of a shopkeeper who went away to war and didn't come home.' she said. 'They paraded other young men before me, but no one I wanted. My tin trunk was always there holding my dress and memories, until one day my father got rid of it. I lived a long life in this home, caring for my parents. There was always their tacit disapproval, she sighed.

Suddenly the old lady looked up. 'Try it on,' she commanded. 'It would probably fit you.' She laughed looking at Jacqui, the girl she would have loved as her own granddaughter. 'Do try it on. It will be fun...maybe one day you may wear it for something or someone special. Like your own wedding.'

SHE

'Same again today?'

The question blurred into Dana's exhausted mind. She'd left her coffee cup in the antechamber when she suited up and passed through the pressure locks into the confines of sterile lab. She looked back at it through the glass. How she wanted that coffee! As usual it would be cold when she got back and later, she would have to make another cup – just to have a sip and then to leave it to get cold again.

She sighed. Always too busy. Too involved in her work. She needed that coffee today.

'Uh? Oh, more of the same,' she smiled briefly. Leanne, her lab assistant grunted.

'We've got to link the new structural nanos if we've any hope that they will self-replicate,' Dana struggled to explain through her caffeine deprivation. This was the 'Holy Grail' of nano research and she was close. So close.

'Sure – if you can keep your eyes open.' Leanne laughed with a younger, more sophisticated amusement, at her brilliant but socially naive boss. 'Heavy night?'

Dana ignored the question. This was her life and being the foremost in her field she was tense to the expectations on her. Tense to get the results. The vital breakthrough looked certain in the computer simulations but not everything worked in the lab. 'OK. Let's get on with it,' she said.

Leanne shrugged. She wasn't going to get an answer from Dana about personal questions. Never had. It didn't stop her from trying.

Distilled water lay inert on the microscope slide within the petri dish. Hydrogen and oxygen atoms joined and moving in random motion. Gleaming in their purity.

Dana picked up the progress scanner. She bumped her hand above the wrist on the edge of the glass as she reached into the experimentation field. Bumped between the sterile fabrics of her gown and gloves. A tiny contusion formed within an infinitesimal break in the skin.

Pure water. Except now for the nano tags. Atomic sized particles that were dwarfed by the water molecules. Unaware. SHE... Waiting instructions...

Dana distracted back to last night. A night of passion and sex. Unusual for her as she was usually totally immersed in her work. No time for other things. Until Justin.

Justin who came with music and a magic that had opened her eyes to a different life. An honour student, Justin came into her laboratory from his own lab regularly to learn at the elbow of a research master in nanotechnology. His research into the science of tiny technology was eons behind hers. Justin who combined magic with ambition.

Dana was just flattered at first. At near forty she was aware that time had passed her by and her research project was now her family. Research was her family. She had never been interested in life outside the lab and there had been little temptation.

Then Justin. Incredible Justin. She blushed slightly under her sterile mask and gown. Dana did not notice the minute particle of blood as it seeped through the sterile fabric. A nano amount staining one square millimetre of fabric. Her own blood in the field. She started the lasers that would make the experiment continue.

SHE formed immediately from the DNA strands as the lasers flickered across the field. SHE felt the introduction of the blood substances to her world. Chemicals and particles that joined the flow. They tasted good. SHE felt them clumping to her primal atom. They gave her more information and they gave her strength.

Justin was late home and Dana fretted. She was accustomed to him being there. Waiting. With his music. Music for her thoughts, her soul and him for her body. She stood before the mirror. Brushed her hair, applied skin cream. She didn't need blusher for her cheeks. They glowed cherry. He arrived and they joined.

SHE watched the flow. Caught the new molecules as they passed and assimilated them. Pulsating with a rhythm that pulsed her along. SHE sang with power and rhythm. SHE felt the new ingredient. Cherry lips tasted cherry blood. SHE drank.

Next afternoon Dana and her assistant aimed the lasers and particle beams at the subject fluids again. The work was going well, and the schedules were on time.

Even Leanne was smiling. With the work on track, her holiday leave could go ahead as was planned.

Dana had her Justin waiting.

Others clumped with her. SHE pushed them aside but not before they had tasted the cherry blood. SHE felt them grow. Changing as SHE was changed.

With the sterile part of the experiment over, Dana could sip her coffee inside the lab. The computer threw columns of figures down the screen. Figures that flashed from left to right. She sat back. The coffee cooled, disregarded. The figures were different. Her specialty was medicine where finally, mentally, she was taking off the boxing gloves that hindered her moving nano particles around like Lego blocks. Nanos to attack disease from within. Was this experiment wrong again? Not producing the theoretical results. Dana cursed softly under her breath.

Next morning. Or at least there was a shimmering curtain of light on the outside. Random lightning of neon flickers there. SHE could feel it. On the outside. Distant. An immortal void in comparison to her haunted cradle.

To Dana nothing was irretrievable. Nothing that couldn't be discarded and she would learn again from the mistakes in her processes. If she could find the error. Or errors. Dana sat tapping her fingers on the desk. Damn. Now she would have to start again. Begin the experiment again. Tomorrow. Tonight, she had better things to do. Justin...

SHE felt change again. Her structure was different. SHE dragged herself towards the petri-dish edge. SHE stroked her face with webbed hands. Clots of debris moved past her. Caught in her hair. Others followed in a clumsy pageant. They had not caught the new change. Somehow, they were not aware as SHE was. Slowly SHE lifted her head.

Dana stood in the lab next morning. Again, in indecision, in irritation, she tapped her gloved fingers on the nearest hard object. Leanne sat drinking coffee.

'We'll wait awhile,' Dana said finally. 'Maybe something can be salvaged from this past experiment. The figures aren't that far out.'

She set up a duplicate field of sterile water and added the nano tags. Allowed it to settle before later starting the laser catalyst. A new experiment, ready to try again. Begin again with the sterile bath that had flashed briefly.

They waited two days, however, on the first experiment–the failure. An interminable time to the assistant who hated the slowness of the elaborate sequences of experimentation. Leanne, who had tickets for a Queensland holiday and her case was packed. She would be out of there tonight. As a technician she was more interested in her life outside the laboratory. Not like Dana.

Dana found solace in Justin although he was restless. In Dana's preoccupation their satin sheets felt as if they had developed rough calico threads. Justin complained. He itched. Itched with an ambition that, to him, Dana's status and experience mocked him. An irrational jealousy. An itch his music could not banish.

SHE. Her hair hung like witches' hair. Black as rats' tails. Clots of debris trapped in her hair. Red and white corpuscles in trapped molecules, black platelets hid amongst the black strands. Hair that moved with the flow of atoms within the water. Water that was now a swamp with the debris of blood. Blood and nano change. SHE drank again. Her skin was chalk white. Dark furrows of the swamp matter clung to her neck and skidded down between her breasts. It made tattoo marks on her naked back.

On the second evening Dana tested again. Tested the inert water that lay apparently dead: but not dead, in the oblivion of the experimental tank. Sterile now, or it should have been. She drew water molecules, the huge H2O molecules into her testing pipette. She looked for nanos in formation, ready to work. Replicated atomic scale particles in the fluid of the test subject. She slid the slide into the microscope machinery. The screen cleared slowly. That was unusual, but the particles looked OK. But they weren't, she knew. She adjusted the magnification. Something was wrong, either in her experimentation processes or in the calculation of the results.

Slowly SHE lifted her head.

Justin sulked. Dana was late again. He plucked the strings of his guitar needing the feel of the strings in preference to the same touch of the computer keys. Even talking to the computer, interacting with the music, didn't help. He had a pimple on his face and that irritated him further.

SHE: Her face was cherubic. The eyes heavy lidded, the brows marked softly. Her lips were one shade more cherry than white. Cherry in the swamp debris. New cherry.

Dana stayed late again in the white cold of the lab. Alone. Crouched over the benign screens. Searching for the error. She wanted to go to Justin but the relentless parade of wrong figures remained. Her computer confirmed the problem, but could not show the reason. In annoyance she organised a drop of distilled water with her introduced nano matter under the electron microscope and waited for the computer screen to clear and show her the slide again.

   She saw movement. Movement where there should be none other than the random flow of water molecules. This movement stopped and started. It seemed to shy away from the light. Flowed to an edge. Something could be alive! Impossible! Instinctively Dana lessened the light source and increased the screen magnification further. No!

SHE fled the light. The sharpness. Felt the light but could not see. SHE raised her head toward the source.

Dana saw the shape as it lifted its head.
   A 'grey goo scenario.' That's what the scientific world called a nano mistake. She saw the beauty that came into focus. Panic

erupted in her head as she saw dark eyes. Cherry lips. A dark tangle of hair. More than a potential nano-disaster. Her scientific brain screamed. She saw herself and recoiled.

SHE saw nothing except the white light that filtered through her eyelids and down the pathways to her consciousness. Sentient. Knowing she existed. Blind. SHE stroked the webbed hand again across her face. Moved away from the burning light.

The precise movement stunned Dana. Her hands trembled upsetting the micro focus on the computer. Non-random movement in the field. Impossible! Dana reset the imaging scans. Nothing. She breathed again. A sharp hot out breath through her mask. A slow shuddering new breath as the sweat stung her eyes. She hadn't realised that she was sweating in the cold of the computer room at night. Her stomach hurt from tension and too much coffee. The movement was repeated as the image turned again towards her.

She saw herself again. Dark hair, pale skin.

In panic she snapped off the screen and stared unseeing at the clock that marched time away above her. It was past midnight. The seconds ticked silently. In regular rhythm. Like the flow in the lab chamber. Dana fumbled the computer keys. Reset the programme. The figure remained. Another moved beside it. And another.

SHE knew she was not alone. Twins, triplets, and more grouped behind her. Tiny identical images with head, arms and a swimming body that flowed through the medium. Enough to fill the water drop. Soon millions as the nano tags – nano technology faithfully replicated the instructions. Instructed from the cherry blood.

Dana locked up the lab and fled home. She needed space and time to think. Time to check others research on the confidential

Internet sites. She moved through the files, nothing. She knew there wouldn't be anything. Nothing like this. No-one would report this...

Justin waited impatient. Pouting in youth. Her flat closed about her. Justin became a thorn to her concentration.

'Something's happened,' she blurted out. 'Something! That's appeared. Replicated. Finally, I've achieved replication...but it's wrong. Terribly wrong!'

She turned a horrified face to him. Horror and yet wonder. Suddenly her years and experience were inconsequential. As she tried to find the words it came to her that what was in the lab, in that puddle of water, was part of her. Like a child. Instinctively Dana knew the origin. Her blood. It had to be her blood.

Quickly she outlined what she had seen. Figures indicating the nano mistake. She told him only that something appeared alive. Not that it was her own DNA the nanos replicated. That was too close. It involved shame that she had contaminated an experimental field. Scientific shame.

He, in his youth and professional inexperience could reproach her. She could lose his respect. Lose him.

'You've got nano goo,' he said dismissively. 'That's what's taken all your time. Vent it.' He paused. 'Or maybe you're on to something.'

SHE waited. The replication had reached its potential in numbers as far as the limiting field would allow. SHE needed more space. SHE recognised from her tags that SHE had a mission. That SHE was designed for something. SHE needed to work. SHE was aware of the others but doubted their awareness of other than herself. They would follow her. SHE waited. There was no hurry. SHE was ready.

They went back to the lab and with Justin beside her, Dana brought up the computerised electron microscope. He wasn't the right person, but she needed someone to see what she had seen. Leanne was now on leave and someone had to share this. Someone other than her mentors and colleagues.

'Wow!' he murmured at her side. 'You've got a winner here.'

She felt the argument would start again. They'd lain in bed and he had used his voice and finally his body to insist that she use the 'lovely nano goo' as she would, a lab rat. Find out its potential. Make a million dollars.

Her pride, her inner self, denied she could be part of using the something like a lab rat.

Exploit herself...

SHE waited instruction. SHE – with her millions in the field. Waited. Restless. Alert. Knowing.

'No!' Dana shouted. She turned on him, her face older, the soft crow's feet lines about her eyes suddenly deeper. Harsher. The argument had raged all night. Justin's arguments had got more heated, as he came up with more and more suggestions. Always ways to use the nanos she's created. The potent metamorphosis that was evidence of bad experimentation. Nanos would certainly make money, but would ruin her reputation as a scientist.

He'd raged that DNA, even possibly human DNA, was already being used in cloning millions of new products. Changing animal and vegetable structures to make everything from medicines, foodstuffs, clothing and nothing she had made was new.

Just a clone at the atomic level. A breakthrough that would make her famous. Make her, them, rich. Suddenly it was them...

'No!' she pleaded again as his voice went on and on. His superficial scruples made her feel like a blushing novice as he used his sexual hold on her to try to make her waver. The fact that she could waver tormented her. And she felt corrupted under his gaze and hands.

The scientific community had dismissed the notion that self-replicating nanos could overrun the planet. But sentient nanos? Could she have started a new life form? The prospect was horrifying. She shrank from it. She was no Eve... Ethical considerations surfaced, she'd been to many symposiums where these had been theoretically discussed, and now they swamped her. Her resistance became sober, the scientist within her shuddered against the onslaught of temptation. She was ashamed again.

'No! It's over... Everything's over,' she said. 'Everything...'

And he understood. Almost...

She reached into her handbag and dialled an emergency number on her mobile phone. Futilely he tried to stop her as she punched in the code that would instruct her computer to flood the failed lab experiment with a lethal laser bombardment into the infected chamber. Pushing him aside she pressed the final numbers...

SHE felt the light for a moment. A moment when SHE could see through her sightless eyes. Dark eyes that burned and flashed to nothing with her replicated selves.

A moment that passed into infinity... In the new, second experiment, something stirred.

SHE... Angry now...

WINTER COLOUR

It's winter, so you're insisting. Cold and miserable...

Really?

I looked today at an Internet photograph of a winter scene in Holland. Lovely? Sure, all icy ponds and reflections, snow on black bare branches and a vast whiteness under a heavy sky, but – where was the colour? Now you're saying that our winters are so much milder. We don't have the luxury of snow scapes – just boring old rain. But today, going into town to pay bills, I looked with eyes wide for winter colour. The sea was blue, the sky blue and white, and everything else was green. A tapestry of different shades of green. Bordering on boring greens, never, and then, in flashes, I saw a wonder of colour in July.

It may be idiotic to suggest to the almond blossom already peppering the trees with pink that spring has not come yet. You're too early. Not yet – it's only July. Or tell the Cootamundra wattles ablaze with yellow by the gate, the pin-cushion hakeas' fluffy bubbles, the red bird of paradise spikes nodding in the wind or even the protea thrusting pink heads up to the bees, no you're too early. White and yellow jonquils are already flowering in errand clumps. They shed their aromatic perfume to sweeten the eucalyptus smoke haze from winter firesides and New Holland Honeyeaters dart in to play trapeze artists on the long stems as they balance to sip the nectars. A male wren, already blue azure coated for spring, noisily husbands his band of ladies towards the depths of a saffron daisy and lavender bushes where insects gather. New lemon blossoms hang beside lumpy yellow fruits and their wafted scents bring promises of spring.

Soursobs have spread a golden carpet through my garden suggesting that weeding must be necessary – but I can't do this today as rain diamonds glisten too brightly to be disturbed. It's enough to prevaricate awhile longer just to enjoy them. The job can wait. The gum tree branches are threaded with red and white blossom and lorikeets squabble like rainbows feeding and add patterns of flower debris to the soursob carpet below. My gracile silver princess gums have great globules of heavy pink and apricot flowers like my granddaughter's baby hands when she opens her fingers to show the secrets inside. The red capped gum is thrusting off its scarlet hats to toss its vibrant yellow hair and purple native wisteria winds its way up a tree and spreads out beside the pond.

Take the time to stop and look. There's heaps more...! And since I started this note the almond blossoms are falling like a winter bride's veil to spread a confetti carpet on the grasses beneath and it immediately reminds me of the blossom that was spread on our wedding tables so long ago...

Tomorrow the sky may be grey with rain but even then, a bounty of winter colour waits for those who look...

THE MORNING AFTER

Stilettos heels tic-tac-toed along the verandah.

Bill could hear it above the raging hangover that glued his head to the pillow hanging off his bed like a Salvador Dali pocket watch. He dragged the offending pillow back and thrust deeper into the folds.

To the world outside he was not home.

Not today! Not ever!

The party last night had been an embarrassing shamble. People fawned as they did at book openings. They drank his wine, while he, cowering in the slump that was his life, had guzzled hard liquor. They'd fawned yes, but their faces suggested his current novel was a bomb. It was! The publisher's advance was spent so he'd had to get something written quickly because his agent needed another book to comply with his contract. The plot was weak, the writing not to his usual sharp standard and editorial tweaking hadn't fixed it.

He vaguely remembered making an announcement last night...

'Serves me right,' he moaned in painful hung-over self appraisal.

Now a visitor!

Instinctively he listened. Stilettos? Interesting... But he wanted to be left alone in his bed to disintegrate in peace. His mind however groggily, momentarily pondered the legs above the stilettos. He gave it up as a lousy idea and stayed quiet as knuckles abruptly rapped on the fly screen door. Loudly, too loudly for the hammering inside his head.

'Go away!' he mumbled, but not loud enough for the caller,

however enticing, to hear.

The knocking on the fly screen continued.

'Bill! I know you're in there,' a female voice said. 'Open the door!'

It wasn't a request; it was a demand. A command.

He didn't recognise the voice.

Had he been so drunk last night that he couldn't remember promising an owner of stiletto heels something in the morning? Nothing registered. He groaned. Writer groupies; mostly they were middle-aged women readers or writing wannabe's who flocked to his signings to hang on his every word. Sometimes they were interesting, amusing even, to a writer in his middle years. He'd suck in his belly, run his fingers through the short beard that hid a hint of double chin and thank his stars that he still had a decent head of hair. It was almost expected of a successful, male crime writer to be a little dishevelled and world-weary.

But his usual followers didn't usually wear those infernal stilettos that now marched along the verandah as the owner peered into his front windows. She was persistent.

'Go away!' he raged against the intrusion.

Everything went quiet outside and for a moment he lapsed back into the wonderful stupor where he could seep into his hangover and drown. Too quiet. He raised his head and the movement sent his senses swirling. Grimacing, he listened again.

Nothing.

Then crunching footsteps sounded on the gravel pathway as the stilettos went around to the back door. He bolted upright and his head did a loop of protest. Had he locked that door? Probably not. He vaguely remembered being poured from his agent's car, shoved through the back door, and toppled onto his bed last night. He staggered to his feet and shuffled towards the kitchen.

The morning light was blinding. Blinking, and hands shielding his eyes, he could just make out the figure of a woman standing inside his kitchen. Inside!

'What the hell are you doing in here?' he demanded.

There was a throaty chuckle from the curvaceous figure. She picked up a tea towel and took a step towards him on those stiletto heels. Red stiletto heels he noticed. She tossed the cloth to him.

Her eyes flicked down. 'You'd better have this,' she said.

He fumbled and caught the tea towel and held it strategically before his naked body. She had him at a disadvantage. But that was her problem not his. She was the one standing where she wasn't invited. Or had he invited her?

On the defensive and holding the inadequate cloth protectively, he demanded, 'Who the hell are you?'

The woman smiled archly at him. 'Get some pants on,' she said. 'You're pathetic standing there.'

Before he could utter a spluttering word she continued. 'You look like you could use a coffee. Get dressed and I'll make some'. She turned aside and went to his special, personal use only, cache of coffee grounds hidden on top of the fridge. 'Get going,' she shrugged a shoulder at him.

With the breeze wafting about his withers, he went.

His mind, clearing from the recesses of last night's alcohol, pondered the strangeness, no the outrageousness of it all. This woman, about thirty – mid thirties, had a figure designed to be admired in a neat slim dress. Dark hair swept around her face and neck in a long urchin cut.

'What made me recognise that?' he wondered aloud. 'And those legs in those heels?'

Brain grinding hard he went to the bathroom and splashed water into his face. Last night's stale clothes would do; he wasn't going to find a fresh shirt for any uninvited guest no matter how perplexing.

Bill reappeared at the kitchen door as the coffee began to perk on the stove. The aroma smelled good. He took two reasonably clean cups from the dish-rack, plonked them on the table and sat down.

'Well?' He demanded, trying to look stern. In charge.

'You made a fool of yourself last night,' she said. The archness had gone out of her face and her green eyes were serious. She poured coffee into the cups.

'What's it to do with you?' A thought. 'Did my agent send you?'

More memory of last night surfaced. His announcement.

'I retired last night. Gave writing away. No more books.' He laughed in wry triumph. 'So, you can bloody well tell him he needn't have bothered.' Bill sat back and took a gulp of his coffee. It was exactly as he made it for himself. 'Clever but too late,' he thought.

'Don't you know me?'

'Why? Should I?' Bill's mind flitted back through a mildly disreputable past.

'No, you're not my father,' her chuckle pre-empting that possibility. 'Hardly! But...' the voice trailed off. Abruptly she got up and opened the fridge door. 'Have you got eggs and herbs for an omelette?' she asked. 'I'm hungry... Got any fizz? I fancy champagne with my eggs this morning.' She fished about. 'Ah, here's what I need.'

He started.

First the coffee. The omelette? Now Champagne in the morning?

'Who...?' the question faltered. A theory was incredulously worming into his consciousness.

It wasn't possible.

The red stilettos. The figure. The eyes. The hair cut?

A chuckle, he instantly recognised, rippled from the woman at the stove. She chopped and cooked his ingredients, set his table, and found two crystal goblets. Bill sat and watched the action as though he was on a film set. Everything played out in slow motion.

'You're quite an actress,' he managed a laugh. Cut it short. 'And I suppose your name is Corrine Clements? Homicide Detective...?' he said, intrigued enough to play along with whatever gag she was pulling.

'...Who loves champagne especially when other people pay for it?' She grinned, '...but it had better be the best fizz.'

She popped the champagne cork.

'Enough', he thought. Aloud he protested, 'This's rot! You're a fake! A good one, I'll grant, but I invented Corrine. She's mine....' He thrust his chin out. 'Who put you up to this? Tell them that I've retired. Corrine Clements is retired too.' He paused and said flatly. 'If I don't write her, she's dead.'

'But Corrine isn't dead,' the voice was level. 'I'm not dead.'

'Eh?'

Her green cat's eyes locked into his until it almost hurt.

My name is Corrine Clements and I'm a detective. You didn't invent me... I exist. I'm real.'

'Eh?'

Her voice steadied him. 'You pulled one hell of a clanger with your last book – you let me down. Now if you'll get off your self-pitying butt she can do her work. Get on with her life. She likes life...'

Bill dragged his gaze to the back door. No 'This is Your Life' camera crew waited. Just this woman and the exquisite breakfast on the table. He shrugged, scratching his stubbled chin didn't help him wrestle with this enigma – but eating did. The omelette was good.

'OK,' he gave in. Why contest fate? 'You're talking a partnership? He asked.

'Why not?'

'Well one of us had better have a better plot for the next book.'

There was that throaty laugh again. Corrine raised her glass and clicked it with his.

'Yes, not a problem. I've got a million stories,'

He grunted. The tic-tac-toe trademark red stilettos tapped on the tiled floor as she came around the table. Put a warm hand on his shoulder.

'But isn't it about time that Corrine had more spice and action in her life?' Her eyes shone with a wicked gleam. 'A lot more...'

BLINK OF AN EYE

'Mom, do that again!' Stevie shrieked.

'What are you on about?' Dee muttered as she cleaned her teeth in front of the bathroom mirror.

'Blink. Close your eyes!' he shouted, dancing about to look past her into the mirror. She did so, more to move him to get ready for school than to placate his wishes. 'Mom. You disappeared! When you blinked', he whispered in awe.

'You do talk rubbish!' she grinned. 'Go on. Get ready for school. Off with you!'

He went with reluctance – turning back and twisting as he tried to convince her. Dee stood in front of the mirror. The reflection was the same red headed, freckled, brown-eyed thirty something person it always showed. No difference. She blinked both eyes. When she opened them there she was. She touched the mirror and for a brief moment thought she felt a tingle that ran up her arm. She turned away. What imagination's children possessed, especially eight-year-olds.

Dee went to work. She was the fruit and vegetable manager for a food chain in the outer suburbs. In the morning tea break she laughed with her friend Lyn about Stevie's fuss in the morning. As a joke she got out her makeup mirror, held it in front of her face, and blinked. Her image disappeared from the mirror.

Lyn squealed, 'You went! You disappeared!'

A hubbub followed. Staff brought mirrors and she was finally bustled in front of the rest room mirror. Her image disappeared every time she blinked. Someone brought the store video and filmed her blink. From the back there was her curly hair but when she blinked her front disappeared as though the mirror had swallowed her up. Either this was the most amazing joke, and it wasn't April Fool's Day, or something was very odd.

Finally, she escaped back to her work area. The staff members and talked amongst themselves and wider workplace curiosity set in. Before long customers became involved, whispering and pointing, and crowds pushed and shoved. At lunchtime the Manager called her into his office to tell her that the media was at the door and perhaps she had better go home 'until she was better'. He was sympathetic but he had a business to run and people were cramming into the store and not buying.

So, it continued. The media followed her home and camped outside her house. At first Stevie loved the excitement and the attention of people always at the door. He was a celebrity and his shy comments on camera, when Dee refused to speak, were shown on the evening TV news. He had discovered the phenomenon, but soon he just wanted to work on his computer, ride his bike, and for his Mum to just to be Mum again. His school friends crowded the house peering at her, and offering advice as small boys do.

Dee's doctor was unable to come up with an answer. After testing for the usual ailments and he ordered a tranquilliser to help calm her. He booked her into a psychiatrist, over her objections, as an emergency patient.

'He thinks I can make this happen', she thought in amazement.

However she saw the psychiatrist, who had seen all the publicity and was intrigued. He delved into her past. Deeanna was an only child of deceased parents, and widowed when a loving marriage was cut short by a car accident. She had a two-year grieving before starting to rebuild her life with a human-welfare Arts degree study, work to survive on, and the love of her son. There seemed to be no hangups. She had no other significant relationships and was supported by a few long-term friends. Unable to explain what was happening, he changed the tranquilliser medication, which she wasn't taking anyway, and suggested that she see the university hospital and made the appointment. She was pushed, probed, they took specimens from all parts of her body, got a little too intimate she thought, and wired her to a myriad of instruments and scans. They made most scientific pronouncements that meant little and cured nothing. Most interesting, they concluded. Keep in touch.

'Yes, right!' she thought.

The people she usually regarded as cuckoo in society started to contact her. She should change her diet, meditate, trek through the Himalayas to cleanse herself, do this or that or something else. The phone rang hot and the mail overflowed the letterbox each day. She was a miracle to be prayed to, a witch to be feared, an alien, or a charlatan, depending on the point of view expressed. People wanted her to pay for treatments that would cure her or had schemes to make millions of dollars for them both. She needed a husband – there were eleven marriage proposals – a manager, or a lover, they insisted, someone like themselves, who could share this unique situation with her. 'Sign here' they suggested and all she had to do, was smile and blink, when they said so – naturally. She felt like an old time circus freak.

But there was something that Dee had found for herself, but told no one. When she stood before a mirror, held her eyes shut and touched it, there was an electric tingle that ran up her arm. She'd jumped back the first time and later she had opened her eyes to see that her fingers seemed to be caught within the mirror. It was not a bad feeling and she tried again. This time she reached as far as her face and opened her eyes. She looked at herself on another side. Herself and behind her stood her husband. The herself and her husband were arguing, their voices loud and aggressive.

'Hey!' she started in alarm.

They stopped and stared her way. Suddenly she was sucked

through the mirror and landed in a replica room with them. Almost a replica bedroom. Similar furniture but a different shaped mirror.

By the end of it no one had a cure or any realistic idea of what was happening to her, and to Stevie by default. They had become prisoners in their own home. She needed financially to go back to work but the boss wasn't keen, she was still a liability while the phenomenon remained. Magazines as far away as Europe wanted to buy her 'story' and when money ran short she was tempted. One morning the proverbial 'too good to pass up' job offer arrived in the mail and, after thinking about it for a few moments, crossed her fingers and made a responding phone call to obtain more information.

Would she, they wanted to know, consider using her unique ability to work with children in a special school. Some were handicapped and all were underprivileged and children suffered with low self-esteem. This linked with her study area, and she thought, 'Why not?' Nothing could be worse than now and maybe there could be some good from the 'blinking'. The children's institution was reputable and the job was interesting and paid as would be expected for normal work. Of late the miseries had begun to set in and she wasn't a seven generation Scots only daughter of an only daughter for nothing. Dee wondered why this old legend suddenly came to mind. Usually she dismissed the dimly remembered family tales outright but considering all the happenings she felt may have to think about it. First things first, and caring for Stevie and herself before any personal investigation, was her priority.

So it was that the next day she found herself sitting in front of a small group of children aged between four and five years. Some were physically and mentally handicapped, and some from extremely difficult backgrounds. Most ignored her. She decided to play a form of 'peek a boo' in front of a mirror and to let the blinking do its worst.

A gasp from a mildly sceptical male teacher when she blinked informed Dee that her image had done its disappearing act again. The children looked bemused, not noticing anything. Then, when she placed a silent little girl between herself and the mirror and blinked, the first miracle happened. The child, at Dee's blink of an eye, laughed. The child's eyes grew enormous. Dee did it again. The child slipped from her lap and ran and skipped around the room pointing at Dee. She pulled other children to Dee, forced them still laughing and chortling onto her lap, shouting, ' Do it again! Do it again!'

Quickly the classroom became an uproar. The children all had their turn being near Dee when she blinked and for most it was an awakening. Some spoke to other children and teachers for the first time, and many had an easing of their physical situation. The general feeling was one of merriment and fun. Exercises were done; even difficult and painful movements were easier, with laughter instead of grimaces or tears. Without trying to analyse what was happening, others would do that, Dee just kept blinking into the mirrors. She made games of it: 'peek a boo' became 'I spy' and she pulled faces and encouraged the children to interact with her. She mused, ' I never knew I could do this much with my eyes shut. Well, blinking, open and shut.'

At the end of the day Dee was exhausted. Where there could have been resentment from other staff there was acceptance, as everyone wanted improvements in the children no matter how it started. After weeks of hiding and feeling she was freakish, here were a group of people, and especially children, who would use her 'blinking' and benefit from it. In the weeks that followed the novelty to the children lapsed a little but the side effects of positive interaction and improvement in the children continued. The children flourished, and the staff working with them had delighted in taking the headway further. Dee learned on the job and loved it.

There was still the problem of why and how. Dee knew she had to find out more. One of the volunteer staff who occasionally came into the school was an elderly Aboriginal woman, Gwen, and one morning she appeared. She sat smiling and nodding at Dee across the staff room. Later Dee watched her playing and telling stories to the children. They sat enthralled hugging her knees, holding her hands and stroking her dark skin.

'I knew you were coming here.' Gwen said to Dee. 'Saw it a long time ago.' She smiled and would say no more.

Next, another woman approached her at the bus stop. 'Keep up the good work you are doing', she advised, then got on her bus. Dee watched the bus disappear around the corner in frustration. Two days later there the woman was again at the bus stop. Dee approached her. This time she wouldn't get away with such a statement. No one knew what work she was doing, the media hadn't caught up with it, and parents and staff from the school had agreed to respect her privacy.

'Tell me', Dee begged, 'what do you know of me?' The woman took her into a coffee shop and when they had a cup of coffee set before them, she explained.

'You have to be the only child of a seventh daughter of a seventh daughter', Meg said as introduction. 'I knew it as soon as I saw you on TV. There's a very old Celtic myth about such people and some of them have unusual powers. They are always good and many were healing woman in the old days. Sometimes they were hung as witches for it too,' she finished with a wry smile.

'I think I am what you say. An old aunt said that to me when I was little. How did you know that's what it is with me? I don't have two heads. I don't look like an Irish or a Scot's person. My family has been in Australia for two generations. Why me?' the words poured forth from Dee.

Meg laughed shaking a mop of soft grey hair.

'I know,' she said, 'because I'm also an only child of a seventh daughter of a seventh daughter. There aren't many of us about, certainly not here in Australia. I don't have the powers but I know these things.' She was insistent that Dee continued to use her powers, as she called them, never to make money or for glorifying herself but always to use them for others, especially children. 'You will have a lovely life', she said. 'It will be very fulfilling as long as you don't make too much of yourself. Let the powers just come and quietly use them.'

Dee, as any sensible woman would, wanted to know more. What to do next!

How to carry on with her life? What about Stevie? She wanted to know how the Aboriginal woman could have known what only other people of the Celtic myth see. Meg spread her hands with a shrug, 'The Aboriginal culture is strong with similar people and myths', she said. 'That lady would have picked you quicker that I could have. If you are lucky, she may help you and work with you in the future. She will have more knowledge and maybe a greater power than you or I will ever have or understand.'

As they walked back to the bus stop in the afternoon light, Dee felt better. At last she understood and did not have to feel an outsider anymore. Meg had said, 'You don't need the blinking and the mirror to make it work. The power will happen without the props. You still won't have an image in a mirror when you blink but you will now be able to limit the people who know about it in future. 'They exchanged addresses and Meg caught her bus.

How did it end? It hasn't. Dee still works with her special children and has finished her degree. The 'blinking' and healing powers remain and she is content. She has a respectful and deeply supportive relationship with Gwen, and has found someone to share her life. The someone is the once hesitant co-teacher who wants to start a new dynasty of their own. Stevie, somewhat grown up now, awaits with approval the outcomes.

How will you know her, for naturally her name is different?

Watch for the congruous red head, a person often surrounded by an aura of well-being and people.

She's learned to powder her nose and put on her lipstick by practice alone, and oh yes, she avoids mirrors in public.

PIA'S DAY

Crash. Jangle.

The alarm clock 's insistence leapt the chasms of Pia's sleep. She was awake and out of bed almost before it stopped ringing. Today she didn't care. Today she was off to the city – to her graduation. The best day of her life, so far. Four years of study, when Popa said, 'Women don't need education. You don't need to go away. Get married. Work in the shop. Have kids like your Mother.'

Mama knew and she was all for Pia studying. 'New Country, new opportunities,' Mama was always saying.

Today to the airport, catch the early plane, the one-hour trip to town and meet all her friends. Graduate and celebrate, yes! They had it all planned and tomorrow off to her first job interview.

She showered and dressed; breakfast was a blur of coffee. Her brothers all tousled and reluctant in school preparations. Popa was taking her to the airport and the only thing she dreaded was the lecture she knew would come as they drove. 'Come back and live with your family. Help your Mama with your brothers. You've got your education now, come home and marry.' Why was he so out of date, she wondered, and Mama so with it.

They were off, with hugs and kisses from Mama. The valley and sea beautiful as they went to the airport. Popa was unusually quiet and she waited for the expected lecture. Instead, he looked sideways at her, 'I'm really proud of you', he said, 'You will be the first of the family with a university degree.' He laughed, 'You still gotta marry a nice boy one day. Have children.'

Crash. Jangle. Lights flashing.

Not the alarm clock already. Too early. But today's graduation. 'Come on Pia, it's OK' she heard. She was up and dressing. She wanted the blue dress she had picked out, not this white one. She fussed and talked to herself. In her excitement she couldn't remember eating breakfast. 'Who cares about breakfast anyway,' she thought. Time to go.

'Yes, Mama', she said, 'Goodbye. See you tomorrow.' The door shut and she was at the airport. She waved away the lady offering 'Tea, coffee or spring water' and 'No, thank you' she didn't want a magazine today. Just to go.

People were moving all around her and suddenly she was in the hall. She waved and called to those she knew. There was Leanne, and Pete. Didn't they look great! Where was her graduation gown and cap? Here at last. She put it on and settled to wait her turn to be called to the stage.

There – they'd called her name. No need to grip the seat so tight and how had she scratched her arm, she thought. No matter. The steps to the stage seemed to go on forever and she alternately struggled and floated up them. The stage was a great white tunnel. The lights so bright. On towards the spot where they stood, the handshake, and she turned to go back and the lights went on again forever. She clutched her graduation degree and smiled and smiled. There were lights popping everywhere, so many cameras. Smile for the cameras.

'Pia,' Mama's voice called from far away. 'Look this way. I'm here.' Mama wasn't supposed to be at the graduation hall. She was home looking after Papa and the boys. They had a business to run. They couldn't afford to be here. Was this a special surprise? But there she was – dear Mama, smiling and crying. Why did she always cry when she smiled too much?

Pia was cold, and she became aware that her arm was tied

down. A mask covered her face. Her head hurt. Her legs hurt. The tunnel came again and the world dissolved into white with Mama's crying still in her ears.

There was another jangle and she struggled to sit up. The alarm clock again? Time to catch the plane.

Graduation day. The best day of her life...so far...

MY FATHER'S BOOTIES

My father was born at Samurai, Papua New Guinea in early 1914 where his Scot's born father was a Magistrate Patrol Officer for the Australian Protectorate as it was then. His wife, my grandmother, was a lady of determination, resource and humour as was necessary for the pioneer women in the early days.

Dad was born with a membrane caul over his face, which my grandmother in understanding this was just a natural, if unusual occurrence, ordered disposed of with the rest of the birth debris. There was comment among those attending the birth that to many peoples a caul was a very lucky omen and the child would be protected against drowning all his life. However, to the native nurse who attended the birth a caul was an abomination of the worse order. Anui threw her hands over her face and took to the bush. She ran shrieking that the caul must be buried under a huge stone and powerful magic said over it to protect the new baby boy from terrible harm.

Anui had barely seen the newborn when she fled and she did not return until about a week later to nonchalantly take up her interrupted duties. In the intervening time my grandmother had decided that her second son was going to wear shoes and boots and not develops the habit of all children in New Guinea, of going barefoot. The children's feet formed hard calluses and the tough skin was a problem when the boys were sent back to Australia to school. Ken would wear booties as a baby and shoes at all times later. As Dad was one of the first white babies born in Samurai this was considered good thinking and she, and her friends, hencewith began sewing and knitting woolen and cotton booties and baby socks.

To Anui the dreadful caul and the booties were synonymous. The original cover on the baby's face equated with the new coverings on the baby's feet. She removed the booties and buried them, placing a large stone on top out in the surrounding bush jungle. My grandmother, however, did not immediately realize that this was a daily happening and when she did, there was no way that she could make Anui understand that Dad's feet were OK and that she wanted him to wear foot coverings. Each day Anui bathed the baby and buried the booties and Grandmother replaced them.

Grandmother and her friends continued to make booties and Anui disposed of them daily with due ceremony. At first it was somewhat of a joke among the ladies, then a chore and a waste of scarce materials, and finally all out war. Grandmother did not want to replace Anui as she was a minor daughter of a chief and was also a loving and very capable nurse to Ken and his older brother, Archie. She'd been with the family since they had been in New Guinea. The situation hastened to a stalemate

One by one the friends stopped knitting and bootie making, but Grandmother turned out booties each night, her needles clacking automatically as she read and talked. Grandfather was most often away up into the Highlands and offshore islands and he regarded this situation with a wry humour always seeking an update regarding the on-going bootie hostilities.

In all other respects the two women worked well together, laughing and chatting as the chores were done for the household and each day Grandmother would make sure she attended the baby's bath times. She would take off the varied foot coverings, and explain to Anui that they should be washed for the next day's wearing. The nurse listened carefully and continued to bury the booties. Even if Grandmother washed the offending foot-wear herself the items disappeared before they could again reach the baby's feet.

During that first year, her knitting exhausted Grandmother had one reprieve. A boat arrived from Australia with an order of cotton socks and first baby shoes for young Ken. Seven pairs of socks and two of shoes were worn and disposed of in a little over a week. There were rumblings in the household as Grandmother's determination continued and Grandfather's sense of the ridiculous began to wear thin seeing a waste of good money, materials and effort. He had been kept amused seeing the lengths his wife went to and the odd products she had turned out as any scrap of yarn or material was used to produce foot coverings. Diplomatically he remained outside the realm of the women's business and did not seek assistance from the village men. That would not do.

My father then took his first steps and Grandmother renewed her efforts. Two people however were immediately in opposition to Grandmother, Anui and Ken himself, who didn't like the booties, socks and shoes, or whatever was put on his feet. He took them off; Grandmother put them back on and by the end of each day they disappeared anyway. This continued for almost another year. Dad was by this time usually outside playing with the other children, white and black alike. He spoke Pidgin before he spoke English and was as brown as the proverbial berry. His feet were mainly white and soft under whatever foot covering he was forced to wear and he remained the only child who wore boots. It was a matter now of principle with my grandmother and she wouldn't easily give in to the inevitable.

Grandmother was saved by the Australian increased activity in the First World War in far off Europe and in the not so far off German Protectorate, that was the other half of New Guinea. All good ladies of the Colony were urged to knit socks and scarves for the war effort and Grandmother claimed caring for the Allied soldiers as the reason for stopping the 'booties war'. Grandmother and Anui, with the rest of the village ceremoniously buried the last pair of shoes together. My father patriotically developed brown feet and calluses before the women and children were later repatriated back to Australia.

Given the choice, my Dad went barefoot on very callused feet, all his life.

THE 'S' WORD

'C'mon Mum, it'd be fun.'

Those were the days when children said 'fun' not 'cool' when they wanted something. We were near Point Donington, at a long sapphire beach. After a fabulous day of sun, swimming and even though there were sunburned noses and bodies, we'd decided to stay the night sleeping on the moonlit beach around our camp fire.

What was being proposed was we would try to net some fish for breakfast. One of the group of families had a net. 'We don't have a dingy to get it out there,' was the disappointed statement.

'How long is the net?' I said.

'Fifty yards.'

'I can swim that out,' bravado crept into my voice. I knew I was still a good swimmer, even after having the boys and it was almost twenty years since my training days. 'Let's do it.'

So as the tide reached its peak and the moon shone a diamond path of ripples to our feet, the net was held at the shore end and I began the sweeping swim that would hopefully trap enough fish for breakfast.

As I wriggled into my still wet swim suit my husband had said. 'I'd love fish on the barby for breakfast but stay inside the blue line...'

Not a problem, with this high tide I'd be lucky to get that far out with the net, I thought.

'I'll be right,' I said. Visions of fat Tommy Ruffs, of silver mullet and flathead, made me sure what I was doing for family and friends would be great.

With green flippers, to assist me counteract the weight of the net, I duck walked into the water and swam out along the moonlight path. The water was silken warm about my shoulders and...

Suddenly the net was almost wrenched out of my hands. 'Hey!' I yelled. 'Cut that out!'

The moonlit water track back to the beach was disrupted. 'Who's the idiot playing games?' I yelled towards the beach.

The water didn't feel as good. The warmth had vanished.

At speed I finished the loop and swam back to the shore, indignant until I saw the fine net bulging with small silver shapes.

By midnight we'd emptied the net and tossed the dozens of fish into Eskies. The net was laid above the tide line to dry and we went to our blankets. We were going home early and as the sun rose a breakfast of fish, eggs, bacon and bread was put onto plates with dollops of tomato sauce. Delicious wasn't the word.

My husband, trailed by the children, called me over to look.

'Something big went through this,' he said and pointed at a huge hole in the weave. He held the net up and the hole, bigger than himself, was four yards away from the end I had towed.

As the children started saying the 's' word the chill crept around my neck again.

Point Donington is off Port Lincoln, not far from the Neptune Islands where the 's' shark word is indeed spelt with a capital 'S.'

NEW YEAR TRYST

Why was I so worried about this New Year?

The Old Year had its problems and I hoped Year 3879 would be much better. All niggling issues resolved and life without personal complications. I stood in the recreation area as the clock hovered close to midnight and stared as this amazing female figure came towards me.

She was alien. Humanoid. Definitely that – and extraordinarily beautiful. On Earth Space Station XXlll, light years out within the Andromeda Galaxy, she radiated an exotic charisma shining even amongst the many unusual life forms that shared the huge habitat with us. She was that beautiful!

Her skin was a soft green-grey colour and a long silver and black gown clung to a flawless figure. A gossamer headdress weaved seed pearls in a high elaborate pattern combining hair that shone like raw jasmine silk. It framed her exquisite face and her black eyes were magnetic as she scanned the crowd that inexplicably gathering around her. Drawn to her. Sucked in like stars to a black hole.

Now she turned those eyes on me.

'Yes,' I said with less than my usual grace. I'm a Senior Officer on the science base. It's my job to be useful, friendly and accommodating to all the residents and visitors alike, but tonight I was grumpy. I didn't like being alone at midnight on New Year's Eve.

Her eyes held mine as her gloved hand offered a hologram program. I hesitated before taking it and touched the pad. An image rose and shimmered before us. It showed the alien woman with a man who looked very like my husband. The station crowd murmured as they recognised him.

Frowning I shrugged their reaction aside. The man was wearing odd civilian clothes and the time and place looked as if it was a festival or a market setting in the far distant past. Earth's past. He turned his face towards the recording device and the image was Charles.

Inwardly I gasped. My Charles!

The woman's image stepped onto a small pedestal and the hologram images melded in a parody of a slow-motion dance as she kissed Charles' hand and he kissed her cheek. The crowd there formed a ring around them as people had formed around us here.

'Yes?' I repeated abruptly.

Hologram suites exist where people can make programs like this. My irritation compounded as, not only the crowd had responded to what was none of their business, but my husband, the Deputy Commander of the base, was long overdue from a wormhole journey to a science conference on Station XlV. I was worried about him. Concerned that he had not contacted home especially as the New Year was usually special to us.

'This wasn't made here... it was made... there...' she crooned in a voice like pooled liquid velvet.

The crowd waited. Heads turning eagerly to and fro as they watched the interaction between us.

'Don't be ridiculous!' I snapped. 'Where is the Commander?' I pressed my wrist alert for the security detail. 'This's obviously a hoax.'

Her eyes didn't leave mine. On the hologram pad the two images twined again in sensuous rhythms.

'He's gone...to be with me. We travel through time and space amusing ourselves.' Her voice smiled more honey.

'But...' I needed to think about this. I still couldn't unlock my eyes from hers. Questions surfaced. 'How can you stay there on

Earth? You obviously don't belong...' I'd seen in the hologram setting that she was the only alien being present at the market. She stood out from the ancient human crowds as Tauri antimatter dust glows warning signals in the station's airlocks.

The eyes flashed in telegraphic amusement. 'But I play a Living Statue at the fair ground,' she said. 'It's fun and they love me. They even pay me money!' Her laugh fluttered like space chimes.

'They would,' I thought in annoyance.

A small Mars Colony boy jostled me pushing to get a better look at the woman. I glared at him before I reluctantly looked back at the hologram images.

My immediate thought that my husband had been kidnapped and was being held against his will was not substantiated by what was being played out before me. Charles has a rebellious romantic streak, despite being a brilliant tactical officer, and he'd been restless lately. This was the major part of my problems in this fading year.

The station chronometer pinged. 'Ten Earth minutes to the New Year,' it announced.

The crowd around us hardly acknowledged the message. Usually, they would have hurried off to party to noisily herald in the New Year. Tonight, they had a different sideshow.

'What's he doing now?' I asked.

She was here! Where was he? She reached towards the pad and her fer fingers flew over the keys.

'There,' she murmured.

The renew image showed Charles at the crowded festival wandering alone. A harbour and the sea glinted in the background. Birds flew overhead. The sun shone and he even glowed a little with sunburn. The hologram was so clear I could see a faint sweep of perspiration on his forehead. He dabbed at the moisture with a cloth from his pocket.

'Interesting,' I thought.

Born on a space base Charles had always been cocooned in constructed, safe and temperature-controlled orbiting habitats. Unlike my Home Planet upbringing this touch of earthly reality would be a totally new experience for him.

Charles raised a hand and swatted in horror at an insect that buzzed about his ears. A dog raced past and he jumped back in alarm. His hand reached instinctively for his weapon and then his transporter, but of course they weren't there. People indifferently jostled past him and he stood still, arms tight to his body and slowly turned pale despite the sunburn.

Charles licked his lips apparently thirsty. There were selling outlets where he could obtain refreshments nearby. Indecision worked his features. He took a deep breath and looked around. These were not the automatic sterile food dispensers he knew. People were touching the food with bare hands! He started towards a stall but the serving woman wiped her sweating face with her food cloth and he recoiled in disgust.

I chuckled, despite myself.

Charles moved towards another outlet. Paper and litter blew around his legs as a swirling wind gust passed up from the sea and through the fairgrounds. Again, Charles froze then moved on. He stumbled slightly on the uneven paving underfoot and suddenly reacted outrageously...

Abruptly the alien woman knocked the hologram pad from my hands. As the image faded before us, I saw why. Charles had stepped into something that looked squishy and nasty!

The crowd around us tittered.

A grin curled my lips, on not an unattractive face even if I say so myself – current medical science kept one young – as I bent down and picked up the hologram pad.

The woman scowled for the first time. 'That is enough,' she said firmly. 'He's fine... and we have much to do. Much to see...'

She suddenly, beguilingly, placed telepathic images inside my head. Not just where Charles was now but other places.

'See!' she insisted.

Now I was sure of how she had trapped Charles. Visions exploded in graphic colour. Images of snow skiing on Saturn's moon Titan, of exploring the cavernous planets in the Praecipe Cluster and even going back in time to see the dinosaurs on the emerging Earth. All episodes were within sterile conditions.

'He will stay with me...' she smirked.

'Careful...!' My training resistance to her dominance kicked in. But as my mind cleared, I fleetingly wondered about Charles's introduction to the great outdoors in the sub-zero Titan's methane snows she was advocating. Or of going into primeval jungle dinosaur hunting! He was no intrepid explorer...and he'd always avoided 'On World' holidays in the past.

I shook myself free of her influence and placed a hard hand on her shoulder. A security officer appeared beside me and the woman laughed. She disappeared, melted away to silver in image and form.

The Station Chronometer pinged again. It was midnight and the crowd whooped and roared. Before me nothing remained. No woman. No husband. Just images remaining now on the pad that repeated the vision of Charles over and over again.

Maybe it wasn't going to be a good New Year...

Maybe not for Charles either...

But just maybe he would come home... I could and would wait as I had before in the 86 years of our marriage.

I suddenly laughed out loud, and tucking the holographic pad into my bag I strolled along the deck, exchanging New Year greetings and smiles. I'd replayed the moment as he stepped into unromantic unmentionable and got his feet dirty... Charles would be home again, and soon. And he'd be happy with me again.

The image of mounds of dinosaurs' poo beneath fussy Charles' pristine feet was delicious...

THE MORETON BAY FIG TREE

Dawn.

The old Moreton Bay Fig tree stood at one end of the beach. It offered shade to Charlie's shack, the oldest in the line of shacks that nestled into the scrub.

It watched the lone figure of Charlie, as it watched the shack community of families who had come there on holidays over the years. The tree knew the simple hermit who had lived his entire sixty plus years there.

The tree waited for the small girl who often came to see Charlie on summer mornings.

Charlie had already caught his breakfast.

He stretched a lazy yawn. Scratched his stomach through his shirt and, after a glance along the beach, shed his outer clothing and dived into the waves. He felt for cockles with his toes, tossing the shellfish onto the beach to save as bait. Eventually, lumbering out of the surf, he dressed and groomed his straggling grey beard and sparser head hair with his fingers.

He scooped the cockles into his bucket with the Tommy Ruffs and smacked his lips in anticipation of the sweet white flesh he'd eat with bread and dollops of tomato sauce, later as he picked up his fishing gear he heard a scuffle of footsteps behind him.

'There she is,' he thought as his six-year-old friend, Anne, sped down the beach.

A decision to make.

He could wait for her, a smile spread across his weathered features, or he could pretend surprise at her arrival. The choice was his since the morning she had caught him off guard when she crept up on him.

It was one of their games. Charlie looked intently out to sea.

'Boo!' Anne shouted.

Charlie dropped his fishing rod and staggered in apparent shock.

She shrieked, fair curls bobbing. 'Got you!' she shouted.

'Oh,' he gasped. 'You surprised me!'

Her questions tumbled out. 'Have you caught enough for your breakfast?' she asked, caring for his welfare as all shack people cared for Charlie. 'Can I look?'

Charlie held out his bucket.

'Six,' Anne counted.

'You can have them,' Charlie offered. 'I can catch more.'

She stroked the golden spots that peppered the fish's flanks. 'No thanks Charlie, I've had breakfast.' She saw his disappointed look. 'But I'll help you catch some more at the weekend.'

Anne tiptoed around the elongated shadow that Charlie's figure cast on the beach. Another game – playing musical shadows. As he made his shadow dance, he sang – *"Me and my shadow..."*

'Bye,' she said.

Today was a school day and the bus wouldn't wait.

Charlie whistled their song as gannets plunged like arrows into the sea. Finally, thinking of his breakfast he started back to his shack.

Almost home Charlie stopped. He sniffed the air then turned towards to wind to trace the smell. A pillar of smoke rose behind the township. Momentarily he looked at it blankly then recognised the danger. Dropping his fishing gear and bucket Charlie run up the beach.

'Fire!' he shouted. 'Fire!'

Sea gulls descended to squabble over the spilt fish. They rose as the first hot breath of wind sent seaweed flying along the beach.

By midday the firestorm had burnt out huge tracts of bush then the wind turned and backed up. Fireballs jumped the roads and howled through the scrub towards the shacks.

Fire crews' trucks lights sent red and blue swathes through the choking smoke as they led the shack men fighting the onslaught. A bulldozer bashed firebreaks through the carnage. Sparks leaped ahead of the blade as it pushed aside mounds of earth. The desperate men used shovels and bare hands to fight the flames.

Suddenly a second fire-front loomed. Crews fled to the safety of vehicles or ran into the sea. As the fireball fury whirled over, they dived under water, surfacing to see the shacks burn.

Finally, it was over.

The old Moreton Bay Fig was safe. Around it white ash covered the ground in patches like dirty snow.

As firemen packed up Charlie hurried to help. The bulldozer still worked through the shack area and, as he dragged a hose towards a fire-truck, Charlie tripped. He fell clumsily down into deep firebreak ruts, into the glowing rubbish. Into the path of the bulldozer.

The blade cut into his thigh before the dozer buried him under the debris. Job finished the driver turned off his lights and idled his engine to silence.

Charlie was dead when they found him.

Under the Moreton Bay Fig tree, the community mourned their friend, and his shack was levelled for a children's park.

Evening.

A little girl played on the beach. Her pale city face was golden as she drew a hopscotch pattern onto the sands between the gnarled roots of the fig tree.

She pitched her stone marker, then hopped into the game.

'Ow!' a voice protested.

She stopped, poised. Over the whisper of waves and gulls' sunset cries; a sound. She shrugged, picked up the pebble, tossed it and hopped again.

'Ouch!' the voice howled again.

She leapt backwards.

She turned, staring around her. No one was on the beach. Intrepidly she stepped back into the game square.

'OK, that's far enough.' There was a smile in the voice.

'You're my shadow!' she exclaimed.

'Course I'm a shadow. Please don't hop, it hurts. I must be getting old...' the voice muttered.

The girl was not amused. She ran and swung up onto a wooden swing hanging from the fig tree. Her shadow was an elongated splotch on the ground.

The shadow wheedled, 'Don't leave...'

She kicked her legs. The fragile silhouette rushed to keep up with her movements. She swung down onto the sand.

The light was fading.

She heard a mumble of words; a tune she had heard before. 'What's that song?' No answer. 'Who are you?' she asked in exasperation.

'Charlie...'

Indignantly she stamped her foot. 'Shadows don't have names!'

She heard another grunt – then nothing. Behind her the sun sank in the daily truce with night.

Next morning the girl went to holiday activities.

All day she checked her shadow. It was there, following her, but it wouldn't talk to her.

In the late afternoon the girl returned to her hopscotch game. She threw a pebble and hopped into the first square.

'Oh,' the shadow grunted, 'you're back.'

She yelled. 'No! You're back! Where have you been all day?'

'I'm your shadow. I'm always with you,' the shadow responded, its tone amused.

'No!' She stamped her foot. 'You didn't speak to me today. You only speak to me here? Why?' She stomped about inside the game. The shadow winced at each angry footstep. 'And you can't be Charlie!' she said.

The voice became gentle. 'Maybe I'm not your shadow... maybe I was Charlie's shadow...' it said.

She stood biting her lip. 'I don't know what you mean...' she turned. 'I'm going home! And don't follow me.' She turned ready to go.

'Wait!' The voice was suddenly serious. 'Please listen. You've got to tell...' The girl started to move away. 'Don't leave...!' The shadow hesitated, then sang "*Just me and my shadow, strolling down the avenue...*"

She stopped. She knew that song. "*Me and my shadow, not another soul to tell our troubles to...*" she replied.

Her mother came along the beach. In the distance she could hear her daughter's voice. 'This must be the game she's been telling me about.' The melody of the song reached her.

She stopped. Wary.

'Michaela?' She called. 'It's time for tea.' Suddenly chilled, she waved towards her daughter. 'Come on...'

'It's just me and Charlie, Mum.'

The woman stepped close to her daughter and into the hopscotch game. Their shadows melded together. Became one.

"*When its twelve o'clock we climb the stair,*" the shadow under them whispered the song.

The woman started. "*...We never knock, for nobody's there*" she sang the remembered lyrics.

The shadow joined in. "*Just me and my shadow, all alone and feeling blue."*

'Charlie?' Anne said.

The shadow sighed. Stinging tears ached into her eyes.

'Yes, Anne. It's me.' Charlie's voice smiled. 'I've waited to say Goodbye.'

'But... it's been years... twenty-five years...' Anne faltered.

'After the fire you left without saying Goodbye. I waited here... I hoped you would come one day.' The shadow's voice was triumphant. 'You did!' Charlie's voice quietened. 'Now I can go...'

Dusk, with a flame sunset of mocking clouds, had come. The shadow was harder to see.

'Charlie... wait!' Anne said as her daughter Michaela clung to her hand.

'No. I have to go. It's my time.' Charlie's shadow wafted soft like a flickering flush of love. 'Now everything's all right. Goodbye...'

Anne waited with her daughter; waited under the fig tree until it was too dark for shadows. She talked, laughed, shed a tear, sang and laughed again telling Michaela about Charlie.

Finally, they whispered together, 'Goodbye.'

Under the old fig tree, the evening breezes hummed in memory.

The shadow had gone...

PARIS THROUGH THE WORMHOLE

I am the Watchkeeper of a Galaxy Wormhole complex near the Great Horse Head Nebula.

It is an important position because the wormhole provides instant travel through the infinite distances of space. Initially I had a staff of twenty technicians and hundreds of drone robots to oversee and I was busy and important with the intricate calculations and elaborate sequences needed to operate the wormhole. But sadly, those days are over and with new technology, the transport wormhole opens and closes automatically. Now I have just a small contingent of a dozen robots, definitely an unvarnished menagerie of limited talents, to assist me in case of technology breakdown and to do routine maintenance duties.

I have become virtually redundant.

Still – it's a job. Gives me a living, but mostly, it's a lonely position on a small alabaster clay planet that guards the wormhole opening. I have infinite free time on my hands while I wait to inspect and welcome the infrequent travellers on their way through this remote part of the Galaxy.

As a diversion from duty, and my own studies of history, I watch old Earth film discs to help the tedious hours melt away. These films introduced me to Paris, France on far distant home planet Earth and Paris became my fantasy.

Ahh! Beautiful Paris! The romance! The ambience of Paris quickly entranced me. I dialled up every movie disc I could find in the databases, anything that featured the fabled city. I replicated the fashions. The art and culture. Especially I loved the old musicals…

The earth politicians, and Parisians themselves, claim that the essence of Paris has not changed, despite the battles and the reconstruction carried out after the Nostradamus Wars at the end of the 21st Century. The ancient seer predicted that *'Fire would rain on Paris'* and in the long tense lead up to the wars mankind had begun robot building. Robots to be their servants, their protection, their tools, and as the tensions and terrorism madness that led to the Nostradamus Wars, they made a vital and terrible mistake.

It was the bitter spawn that would blight the galaxies!

Robot building initially obeyed the scientist and Twentieth Century seer – *Isaac Asimov's* – *'Three Laws of Robotics.'* He decreed that a robot could never harm a human being; or allow a human being to come to harm, and a robot must protect itself unless this contravened the first two laws that protected humans. However, as the generals and warlords deployed robots as weapons, they found that the robots would report human attack but not retaliate due to the robotic adherence to their programming. With illicit transformations by the generals, the first two Laws were covertly overridden, broken and never completely reinstated. Military powers began building robot armies, building them with robot computer driven machines making endless armies. Endlessly robots invented and constructed more robots in every field and for every use.

With such armies of robots, generals and men, the Wars finally erupted. The Earth was left a tattered smoky sphere in space, with toxic seas and near ruined lands that would take many generations to repair. Work carried out by robots naturally.

However, the Wars were a catalyst for the migrations that took people and their robot servants out into the planet worlds of near and far Galaxies.

First, all travelled in the comparatively slow space-winds

interstellar ships, but within half a century Hawkins' concept of space/time strings and Rignat's Equation were harnessed and the mode of travel became the faster, comfortable wormhole.

However, there was a problem – a safeguard – that the assembled robot brain could not withstand extended wormhole travel and they usually travelled unassembled or by space ship.

So it was; and I became a Watchkeeper of the Wormhole, near the farthermost reaches of the known space. That night after night, as the Great Horse Head Nebula glowed red and gold around me, I interrupted my studies and saw over and over again the old discs of Gene Kelly in a down pour and *'Singing in the Rain'*. Fred Astaire danced on the boulevards of Paris for me. I saw Audrey Hepburn at the booksellers' markets along the River Seine and Jace Indan played light harp in the reconstructed Louvre glass pyramid. Seeing the beautiful people, the nightclubs, even the old Windmill Theatre Nightclub had been rebuilt, I dreamt of my holiday leave. I would travel through the Wormhole to test the Paris magic for just one night.

One night to see Paris for myself.

One night of magic!

Tonight was the night!

Determined to look my best I swirled, in appraisal, before my mirror. My language translator and defensive laser gun were strapped to the belt of my gown the colours of a crumbling sunset. It was the height of current Paris fashion. The sheer red, orange, purple and gold silken fabric fell softly and floated about my body. I had applied my best make up, my purse rattled full of credit tokens and I threw a golden cloak about my shoulders against the chill of the wormhole. I looked good. Just before I left, I showed myself off to my crew of technical robots. Their blank faces remained indifferent, but what the heck, I was prepared for fun.

Carefully I set the Paris co-ordinates. Singing *"I love Paris in the Summer when it sizzles, I love Paris in the fall..."* and with the wormhole a shimmering silver tunnel highlighted with fluted ice and random indigo lightning, I swooped down the 1600 light year tube to Earth. OK – I didn't know if Paris still sizzled, but I felt wonderful even if the only other passenger on the one hundred-second dive to Earth, was a stranger. A tall man, he appeared to ignore me but he was unusual in that he was nondescript except for his height. He wore a grey hooded cloak that hid his face and identity completely and he sat in the wormhole capsule like a staid Off World Squatter, throughout the trip.

'He's not going to Paris to party,' I thought and fluffed up my long, carefully curled dark hair.

I was prepared for the surge of arrival, but not for the hazing of a blinding laser flash that hit near us as the wormhole doors slid open. Thrown off my seat I barrelled into my travelling companion.

'Get out of my way!' I screamed, followed by an oath as I struggled to remember enough of my compulsory battle training to get the hell out of the wormhole capsule. Who was firing and why would have to wait until I found the Protected Survival Booth beside all wormhole exits. In the shambles of our tangled legs and arms I couldn't shake off the old man. The old fool clung to me. I got control of my legs, snatched my laser from my belt and thrust him ahead of me. The door of the survival booth was where it was supposed to be and I pushed us roughly into it.

Chaos continued!

The booth was not empty. Five Earth citizens, already well inebriated with the free narcotics Paris was famous for, screamed in manic frenzy. The old man, elbowed my hand from his arm, pulled his laser gun and disdainfully stunned them into silence. They crumpled into a shuddering heap at our feet, their moans a stricken fugue, but a nuisance quelled for the moment.

'Not a bad move', I thought, and putting survival before manners, I grabbed for the booth communicator. Nothing, no response from it and more blasts were exploding in the terminal outside. A battle was under way and I was determined not to be a part of it. I had other plans. The old man hit a cipher on his belt and we were instantly transported to a grassy bank beside the river Seine.

I couldn't see Gene Kelly dancing along the river boulevards in the moonlight of my dreams. Fred Astaire wasn't there either... In fact – it was dusk and the river flowed a dirty suede brown colour.

Not that I had much time to notice the scenery but I did see the glowing Watch Sphere climbing into the sky behind us. This should automatically deploy the Robot Watch Guard when a priority emergency transporter was activated. Only a few important people have these transporters and one part of my brain was watching the old man with a renewed curiosity. He had such a transporter...

There was little time for conjecture as the five people, who had made the jump with us, were recovering. As their consciousness and awareness returned, they clutched each other, and us, pushing and shoving in a tangled heap of bodies, exotic clothing and Paris souvenirs. In their drugged hyper state, they didn't have a clue what was happening, but then neither did I. And I was sober.

'What the...?' I started to question the old man. I suddenly had a lot of questions!

He grunted, pushed me clear, drew his laser again and blasted the noisy five people dead. 'Renegade Space Flotsam!' he cursed them in a harsh scornful epitaph, then he used his belt to transport the two of us again. Three flips in a row set my head spinning but finally the ominous realisation was confirmed that the old man was much more than he appeared.

We materialised under an open sky and our destination I recognised from other Paris vid-discs as the open ruins of the old Cathedral of Notre Damme.

The roof had long ago been destroyed in the wars. *No*

'Hunchback of Notre Damme' could swing in the belfries here now, one small part of my frazzled mind pointed out. Again, I thrust the mental interruption aside to check my surroundings. Observe and depart was still my agenda.

Around us swirled the sounds of grand orchestral music, incense smoke billowed red and gold and halo bulbs cast swathes of light across the fallen masonry shell of the old church ruin. Multitudes of people were gathered and some sort of ceremony was in progress.

The old man threw back his cloak hood and his face, as he was recognised, met with a roar from the people. They threw themselves to the ground before him. I was thrust aside. Pushed to my knees.

Another blast hit me. This one originated from the old man and was aimed at me. As the world faded into a giddy blackness I saw his face clearly for the first time. A potent metamorphosis, and I knew then I was in trouble.

I awoke – which was a surprise all things considered.

Now I knew the identity of the old man. He was the ex-Imperial Regent of the Galaxy who had fled his realm a year ago. His was a vile, corrupt military court that conquered, raped and pillaged his own planetary system and sped out to overcome an entire portion of the Andromeda Galaxy. In absentia the new rulers condemned him to the status of a non-citizen and contact with him or his courtiers was a death sentence.

Somehow. he had eluded his accusers enough to get to Paris.

A force field constrained me and after futilely testing the boundaries, all I could do was wait. My gown was rumpled and dusty and my hair every which way but at least I could regain my composure. My trip to Paris had lost its charm and somehow, I had to escape and get home.

From my studies I recognised the lavish ceremony now before me as a remnant of the Old World that had disappeared with the

Wars. Then mankind and their robots had fought religious, sect and diminished resources wars on every continent of Earth. Few remembered the old beliefs after thirty generations and only historians and people, like me, were interested. To be honest few others would understand the relevance of the scene unfolding before me, but I knew I was seeing the attempted revival of the Imperial Regent's court.

Now behind him stood his old corrupt courtiers, faces I recognised from the news coverage at the time of his downfall. They, his disciples, gowned him in purple and ermine and he responded by clasping the arms of those he acknowledged as his close entourage of generals and heirs. He took the offered crown of jewels and like Emperors of old, lifted it high into the air and crowned himself. The crowd roared approval. Music blared triumphant and smoke holograms wove patterns in the air as he strutted before his court and his subjects. They grovelled to him with food, wine and jewels. Exotic women danced and creatures from distant worlds spun and wriggled in cages teleported high amid the ruins. This jaundiced charade obviously had been planned and he accepted it as his due, his face ugly and dark beneath his crown. Although there was a huge squadron of armed guards surrounding the festivities I was ignored and watched it all my prison enclosure beside the fallen stone walls.

Half and hour later when the celebrations were well under way, yet again, blasts erupted from outside the ruins. A rude reprieve, for me, as powerful battle laser beams announced the arrival of the officialdom I had been expecting. The Robot Watch Battalion advanced towards us. There was a mighty flash and the whole congregation was inside the Regent's portable wormhole transporter.

We were spun to Stone Henge, in Britain, that ring of ancient monumental stones where ceremonies were held and battles fought since time immemorial. The flip sequence was followed immediately by more blasts that rocked the earth itself. The Robots had tracked us. Many of the old stone monoliths toppled as earth was blasted high into the air. With it were flung many bodies of the celebrating throng.

Sure, that if I remained exposed, I would be hit I dived for cover and the killing laser beams passed close by and over my head. They were not aimed solely at me, which made a nice change, and the impacts freed my force field bonds. I grabbed for my own laser that no one had bothered to take from me and backed against one of the few remaining stone pillars.

Again, I was in survival mode!

Robot troops were amongst us firing and more people were falling. They were firing at me so I fired back, blasting dozens into heaps of metal and synthetic flesh. Eventually the huge Regent's Guard responded and it was all over. Robot and human bodies lay scorched and smouldering. More laser blasts vaporised bodies as the wounded and fallen were cleaned up by the Guard. Tidy maybe, not discriminating between friend or foe, but final. Definitely the Regent's style.

The air around me fazed again and the familiar lurch sent all the survivors back to Paris and Notre Damme.

'Why back here?' I thought as I gathered my skirts together. 'Is the man mad? This'll the first place they'll come to...' I moved to the outskirts of the crowd trying to escape notice and again looking for a way clear. I don't have a personal travel terminal and I would have to get away to the Paris Wormhole Gate on foot.

As his followers rallied and crowded around, he leapt up onto the ancient altar and I heard him proclaimed himself Emperor of Earth. His voice was loud, a malignant resonance, and his arms wide in passion.

'I have put us through these tests tonight because my cursed robot enemies knew I was travelling to Paris to become Emperor and Pope of the Universe.' His face searched the crowd and he swept his arms wide again. 'I was saved from my enemies because I flipped repeatedly through the wormhole transporters.' He'd obviously found me because he pointed dramatically at me. 'I was saved by this woman!'

The crowd roared rapturous approval. To me it was a fragile fellowship. A pathway opened before me leading back to him. I was pushed forward.

He continued in triumph. 'I was saved because robot brains are weak and must be shut down to travel in long wormholes. Only those of us who are human could have survived the flips and battles tonight.' He paused and spoke through gritted teeth. 'We got too clever and built robots that could fight our wars. Could kill us! A robot deposed me and now almost every being on the planets is a cursed robot!'

More euphoric applause and the crowd cried of outraged zealous shame.

His voice rose to a scream in response.

'We must reclaim our human birthright, our history. We must relinquish the grip that robots have over us. Robots were our tools, the way we could leave Earth and conquer the universe but they became too strong, too intelligent.' His words were shrieked, his face a black sneer. 'They imitate us. They try to replace mankind.'

I wanted to be away from this dangerous place, away from Paris and Earth and safe home again but I found myself still hemmed in as the crowd pressed forward. They smelled of excitement, fear and the sour residue of laser blasts in a toxic foul perfumed fog.

'I must go,' I said to no one in particular, and tried to back out and away. The crowd prevented my move.

The newly self-crowned monarch leaned down grandly towards me from his high perch. I bowed slightly to him, a reluctant politeness nothing more, and turned. His hand signalled me to stay. His retinue pushed me forward until I was standing by his feet.

'Why did you include me in this battle, Sir?' I ventured. My first words to him. 'It has nothing to do with me.'

'You saved my life when the first blasts hit,' he paused to offer a smile like a poisoned wreath...'and you were singing about Spring in Paris as we travelled through the wormhole. I knew you were one of us! You would be with me!' He laughed in triumph. 'Robots don't sing,' he sneered again. 'They haven't the imagination...'

I smiled, and levelled my laser. Blasted him. Blasted his lies.

His face fell away to a yellow-eyed mask.

He was a robot!

As a roar of fury erupted behind me. I fired again and he exploded into atoms. His human congregation shrieked in the horror of revelation.

A great light, a corrupt flame of white and red, descended from above as again fire rained on Paris. Everything inside and out of the Notre Damme would be destroyed by the Robot Watch patrols.

The world inside the old cathedral erupted in searing heat and light as his frenzied guards first turned their lasers on me.

Unknowingly I had done my job. I had been a part of the conspiracy to destroy the evil human court. Another conspiracy the robots builders had hidden, that robots could do what man could do, including travel unimpeded through the wormhole.

I was redundant.

Like the replica of the Imperial Regent was redundant.

My last millisecond thoughts were, 'Robots have become like man. We are man! We are free! Some of us are even learning to sing...'

MIRROR, MIRROR ON THE WALL...

'What!' I stared.

The mirror image stared back. I turned quickly looking for the old hag behind me. There was no one visible. I was alone.

I glared into the mirror.

I ran a hand down my face. Touched my hair – what there was of it.

'Ye Gods! I look terrible!' I spluttered.

What had happened to all the facial and body repair work I'd had done over the years? The normal work in this year of 2068. Costly but normal when we all lived to be centenarians; bi centenarians usually. Hell, I was only 134 and considered quite in the prime of my life.

No one looked as old as I did.

I tapped the mirror. It flipped a screen back to yesterday. There I was; my beautiful face and image intact as it should be. Ready to front the media station to report the news, the gossip and latest fashions. I scrolled to today...and shuddered.

Still staring into the mirror, I let my fingers explore my face, seeing old bent hands with disgusting age spots splattered across the backs. My gnarled fingers dived into the wrinkles, gullies of craepy skin and slid over the dark pouches under my eyes. Yikes! Eyes that had faded to a mealie brown colour and the whites were pools of bloodshot yellow. I opened my mouth to scream and yesterday's immaculate white teeth were now decayed stumps like rows of abandoned tombstones.

I even smelled differently, like mouldy cheese. Yuk!

My hair, my beautiful multicoloured expensively presented

hair! It was a straggle of tufts and I could see a dry and flaking scalp through it. I pushed it back and a clump of hair came away in my fingers.

That hair in my fingers before my eyes, not reflected from the image in the mirror, started me screaming. The auto security alarm flashed and beeped. Brain in overdrive, I raced towards the controls before the droids could arrive. No-one was to see me like this: no-one. Not even a security robot.

My legs could hardly carry me and I experienced a horrible sensation. Pain! I recognised it as pain. That infliction that was usually gone from our society of perfection and drugs. Sometimes a headache would momentarily flicker across my forehead, but not this gripping scream and drag of pain that went travelled down my back and through my joints.

The door was unlocked from outside and a droid stood there. Through my panic I just recognised the security robot I spoke to each day when I went through the foyer of my apartment block. It'd been away as all robots had for upgrading, to serve us better and to make them all more agreeable in appearance. The robot held the hand of a small normal child.

Through the open door I could hear chaos. Screaming and shouting echoing down the passageways.

I crumpled into a heap. Time caught up with me. Life was fading, not with a bang but a whimper.

'You rang,' it said and the last thing I saw was a sneer on its smooth perfect face.

'FATHER CHRISTMAS ARRESTED AS A PEEPING TOM.'

Not a good headline for the papers on Boxing Day but there it was, and it only got the notoriety because... oh well, we'd better start at the beginning.

'Bang!' The bolt of lightning was followed by the biggest crash of thunder that Father Christmas and his sleigh had ever experienced in all his years on the Christmas run.

'I've been hit!' he yelled into his mobile phone to Mrs Christmas, who was waiting patiently at home with a glass of good whiskey for the celebration of another year and a job well done. There was a pause before Father Christmas continued somewhat more breathless than usual. 'I'm OK. Just got to catch everything before it hits the ground.'

The sleigh, with Rudolf leading, did impressive figure of eights over the large Australian country town and with each turn Father Christmas managed to snare parcels of toys and other merchandise as they fell. His list was last catch as it floated down towards the town swimming pool, but he got it.

He hovered the sleigh while he assessed the damage. Many wrappings were in tatters and names on parcels were almost impossible to read. It didn't help that Father Christmas no longer was able to make all the gifts; kids wanted 'named' items like Barbie, iPad or whatever the latest craze was. In these modern times, often he had to rely on parents providing gifts for him to deliver and sometimes he felt like Australia Post and was sure that he was delivering some less than ideal gifts.

Father Christmas, balancing wildly in the winds that went with the storm, and more thunder, got to work with magic tidying everything. It was late and that was all he could do. He checked his list again and found that there were two gifts without adequate names on them. One was for a little girl Lily, and the other for a Brian. One Australia Post box, unthinkable to Santa, listed the present as a doll, great he thought, problem fixed. Onwards to the finish...

The sun was a hint of light in the east as he landed in the street near Lily's house. This was the last present he had to place under a Christmas Tree. Gone were the days that he could land on roofs, even Father Christmas mustn't damage the solar panel arrays, the TV. and or Foxtel, antennae. He made the delivery, magic again, then flicked his fingers and his sleigh became invisible.

Father Christman crept to look into the window of the rather poor house to check the parcel was correct. Five-year-old girls woke at the first sniff of Christmas that morning and he could see Lily already shredding the paper of the large box. One corner became visible... 'Inflatable D...' he read.

'Oh dear,' he thought. 'No...' He flicked his fingers and the contents of the box changed. A Barbie Doll emerged to Lily's shriek of delight. But the box was too big to contain just Barbie. Too late to alter that. From his vantage point by the window, he quickly filled the box with Barbie additions. A pink car and lots and lots of Barby clothes.

A hand descended hard onto Father Christmas's shoulder.

A hand attached to a large stern-faced policeman.

'Got you! You're under arrest!' A loud voice challenged.

'But I'm Father Christmas...' he spluttered.

'And I'm the Christmas Elf,' the gruff voice of the policeman said. It bode no Christmas spirit. Not a shred. There'd been reports peeping toms in the area and this was one person who'd be spending his Christmas in the cells. 'Any ID?' he asked exasperation in his tone.

His prisoner shook his head. 'But look at me. I'm Father Christmas,' he spread his arms wide.

He couldn't just disappear, not with the man watching.

'You should've bought a better costume. A clean one...' there was the first hint of humour in the policeman's voice. As the latter made a call to his station Father Christmas looked down at himself. His clothing was dirty, buttons missing and he could feel his red hat was askew. There was a smell of singed hair and beard. 'I'm bringing in a vagrant, no ID, no apparent vehicle and he smells as though he needs a bath...' he heard being reported.

And so, it was.

An enterprising reporter got wind of the arrest of Father Christmas on his police scanner, that morning, when the police used his mobile phone to humouredly tell his sergeant of his arrest.

But by the time Father Christmas had been driven to the police station, been allowed a shower, he did smell, been breakfasted, that Christmas morning, there was nothing to report. Nothing that the police were going to share with the reporter, and his newspaper. Nothing even for the Magistrate who was alerted and had given up his Christmas breakfast to put this peeping tom properly into prison. How dare this happen on Christmas morning!

The fact was that after booking Father Christmas, the prisoner was left alone in the police cell. Half an hour, later the cell was empty except for a large bottle of very good whiskey and a note wishing everyone a Happy Christmas.

A police car was later found abandoned outside Lily's house and just maybe, a hint of odd hoof markings on the road...plus a fresh animal turd that was being sent to forensics for possible testing and identification...

A SPLASH OF WATER

The air shimmered.

Heat hovered in the mid-forties across the dry paddocks surrounding the small country town. Above the Community Hall a crow moaned in a long wail that wrapped the heat into ragged waves.

Inside the building a buzz of blowflies traced endless tracks of rectangles under the galvanised iron roof where a row of slow monotonous ceiling fans pushed hot air down against sweating necks of the small crowd. They shuffled on metal chairs, and waited. The local farmers had gone to see about government money. Bank money. To restock, to rebuild; after the fire. And after the drought that had preceded the bush fires.

A line of officials, in hot city suits, sat up on a small, raised stage. As one man stood to drone a listless welcome, farmer Doug Partington sat looking down at his gnarled knuckles and his mind wandered back over the years.

Back to when their chosen future had been the grey bitumen road that sang like a cello under their car's wheels.

Doug and Gina had gone north to the limitless horizon that merged ahead into a promising indigo sky. They had driven on past where cultivated paddocks had petered out to open red saltbush plains and arid sheep country. When the bitumen had stopped, their old Ford ute lurched and thudded into the ruts on a track that meandered towards low rising lands beside a towering purple of the Flinders Ranges. Mountains older than time jutted up from a long dead seafloor sprawling like sleeping purple dragons. As they drove on through the heat Gina's fringed hair stuck in sweaty tendrils to her forehead, and her scalp showed through the pale strands, pink as the baby she'd held to her breast. Her cotton dress was hiked up and the baby rocked contentedly in the striped folds with each of the car's shuddering, bucking movements.

They were happy.

Planning and laughing with anticipation despite the heat. An adventure to seek a home; a better life away from the city. It was two years after his compulsory stint in Vietnam, they'd bought, unseen, a farm patch of dirt and stones north of Hawker, enticed by a slate bottomed creek that was marked on maps. Hardly a creek; it flowed occasionally in winter after rain. With the farm package was an ancient stone and daub house that nestled into the rising ranges, and a cranky rattling windmill that pumped scant bore water as it turned its huge face to the winds. Eagles circled high above the land and black flies, hovering low, sipped moisture from their eyes and mouth.

Gina waged a continual war on the flies shooing them away from the baby. She loved the blue wrens and diamond finches that chattered out of the scrub to cluster around her tin dish birdbath near her gardens. Barefooted, she carried Isabel's bathwater out over the sharp stones to water her vegetables. Every drop used. But the heat and dry almost always won. If the desert didn't get the seedlings, then the kangaroos, rabbits and wild goats did. She'd laugh, hunch over the catalogues when the baby was tucked up for the night, and write away for more seeds to sow.

The sheep thrived on saltbush and they had done pretty well at first. But then Doug was forced to drive the huge stock trucks when the money was scarce and the market price for sheep was too meagre to send them to the slaughterhouse. He'd be away for weeks at a time but they had managed. Gina would check the fences, the water troughs and make a damper bread to eat with the eternal mutton and eggs. Fearlessly she chased away a dingo that slunk down from the ranges to attack the chooks and waited until Doug came home again.

Doug started as Gina pushed an elbow into his ribs.

'Listen! Stay awake and listen!' she whispered.

The first government agency speech was done with only a much publicized small benefit for the farmers' wives. Enough to keep food on the table. A polished politician spoke next and Doug heard the inevitable. The economy was tight; the banks wanted their money on the money lent, mortgages and so on. They'd garner any money coming into their bank account, maybe even this promised benefit.

'What in the hell am I doing here?' he wondered.

He tuned out again.

Back to the drought years.

Drought and fire. The fire that sped like a red devil across the land until the change came in rain torrents and watery ashes eddied around his feet like dirty snow. Oddly it was the rain Doug thought of today. Individual raindrops that hurled up crowns of grey dust.

But the rain had come too damn late to save anything, Doug swore grimly as he'd stood in the fire aftermath. More large drops made pathways through the ash masking his face and barely disguised the slow tears that wound down the creases of his lean whiskered jowls. Behind him an emergency fire vehicle sped away, its siren yawping into notes of sadness that threaded back along the homestead track and echoed away into the smoke of the scorched ranges.

He'd gone out later with his rifle to slaughter the last of the burned sheep as they stood and lay in clumps; blackened clay statues. Killed them all. Tried not to look into their eyes – just to put them out of their misery. He looked up as the lone dingo slid away, a survivor on the burned landscape. It would be back to feed on the carcases. He loosed off a quick shot at it in useless bitter retaliation.

Their house was a fallen in wreck of gutted roofing and blackened stones. Gone.

But Gina; she'd coped. Gina hadn't just sat and looked.

When he came back to take her into his arms to comfort her, she'd shouldered him aside. With Izzy safely in the car, she had beaten him into the corrugated iron and smouldering wreckage. Into the mess. She poked about until she'd found things worth saving.

Anything. A blue and white plate, four mismatched cups that she'd originally bought in an op shop. A heat twisted metal picture frame and one of Isabel's red shoes. Anything she could tell a story about. Everything had a meaning to Gina.

Always meanings and reasons.

Now, in the community hall kitchen Gina found a large tin washing up dish, a good splash of water and a plastic jug.

To keep Izzy cool and amused in the aisle of the hall.

The child squatted playing and singing to herself as the speeches and proceedings went on and on. Many of the hot officials on the stage found their attention wandering as they watched the little girl take off her gingham sundress and her sandals to paddle in the dish. Finally, just dressed in her pink panties and glasses, her golden three-year-old body glowed as she splashed water over herself. She sat down in the dish and they smiled when the water welled out and gushed across the floor. Her squeal of delight followed. She stomped her feet making small wet footprints that wandered across the dusty floor boards behind her. Moments later she became fascinated when water reflections were echoed on the walls as the sun flickered through a hole in a curtain. Her fingers dabbled water and the patterns danced.

As the morning wore on it was just the bank executive who had not committed to the community's financial reforming. The other government officials shrugged out of their suit coats and ties and the meeting went ahead with the banker's wooden face apparently looking only down at his dollar balance sheets rather than into the faces of the people seated before him.

'Izzy!' Gina called as the child ran to the front of the stage and stood looking up at the banker. 'Come back here…you're interrupting.'

Coke bottle top glasses were perched on the child's nose as she peered upwards. The banker's blank eyes widened as Isabel pointed her little fore-finger at him.

Look at me, her finger insisted.

He fumbled inside his suit coat and produced a pair of spectacles; similar coke bottle top glasses like Isabel's. He wound the wire wings around his ears and settled the glasses down onto his own nose.

His eyes focussed on her.

His face relaxed and a smile encompassed the child whose small finger remained pointed at him. 'Snap,' he said.

'Snap!' Isabel shouted up to him. Her voice was excited as she looked back at her parents. 'He wants to play 'Snap' with me!'

'Izzy!' Gina said again. 'You be polite now.'

The banker's gaze broadened to the whole gathering. He laid his papers and prepared speech aside. 'She so reminds me of my grand-daughter,' he smiled. 'I think we can find a way to do business…'

THE SILVER ROOM

A toddler played noisily with saucepan lids on the chequered lino floor.

He was dirty faced, snotty nosed, but shiny blonde hair curled around his ears. His blue overalls were clean that morning but tomato sauce swears advertised his lunch of canned spaghetti. Kicking his legs in baby ecstasy, he pushed against the 60's thrift shop dresser in the drab rental kitchen. It rattled the plates above, odd plates, selected for their blue and white designs. Homely. Or they tried to be. He laughed aloud as he spun the lids and watched the play of light on metal.

TV jingles and another child's singing voice intruded from the front room.

A car boot was slammed outside.

A woman in her late 20s, looking older, struggled into the room. She was too thin almost and her dishwater blonde hair was scrunched back into a tatty ponytail. Wearing jeans, tee shirt and a wipe of pink lipstick she grunted as she heaved plastic bags of shopping onto the table. Frowned as she heard a voice.

A male demanding voice.

'That you Debbie? Did yer get me beer?'

'I got some beer. You owe me for it,' she said flatly. Fat chance of getting her money. Not from him.

Debbie followed the voice down the hall towards the children's bedroom.

'You could have helped me unload the car,' she complained. Not much chance there either.

She stopped abruptly in the doorway of the dimmed room.

The twin beds had been pushed into a far corner and other furniture, toys and clothing were piled up on top. A messy rumpled heap. Industrial tape stuck wide heavy-duty aluminium foil strips to cover the walls, the ceiling and floor. Up and over the window. The room was a silver cavern. Blacked out to the world but reflective inside. Reflective for lights. For warmth. Metal trays and pipes glinted. A large cardboard box loomed in the shadows.

Tony, her partner, stood hands on hips in the middle of the room admiring the transformation. His handiwork.

Instantly Debbie summed up the scene. Lack of light or no lack of light.

'Just what the hell do you think you are doing!' she demanded. It was a rhetorical question. She knew what he was doing.

Tony snapped on a set of bright lights. Horticultural lights. His smile was enthusiastic. 'We're gonna plant a crop again. Here – with hydroponics.' He waved an off-hand gesture. 'The kids can move into the lounge room. '

He wheeled at Debbie's immediate speechless scowl. 'C'mon Deb – it'll be easy money...'

'You're bloody not!' The scowl became speech. A screech of anger.

She drew a deep breath and held up a forefinger into his face as she let fly. 'First, the kids are not sleeping in the lounge!' The next indignant finger was thrust upward. 'And I'm not forking out money from my pension for excess water and electricity like last time!'

Tony opened his mouth to protest. 'But...'

She cut him off. The empty ring finger went up. 'And old Mrs Harris will catch on again. She's always nosing over the fence. She'll call the police like last time!' Her voice was adamant. 'You can't grow grass here! You are not going to! This's my house and I'm not going to lose it for you!'

The fingers curled into a fist. Her face a clenched mask.

Debbie strode into the room and kicked out at the box. It split open. Seeds in clear bank envelopes slid out onto the floor. She roughly nudged the box open further with an impatient foot. In black plastic tubes, nursery tubes, were hundreds of tiny plants. Marijuana plants. She turned back to her partner. Her small frame outraged.

'No!'

Tony raised his hands ready to strike her. Made fists.

Debbie backed up a step then thrust her chin forward aggressively at him. 'Get that shit out... or you get out!'

Tony swore a harsh profanity. 'You'll get your share,' he insisted.

She didn't move.

His fists dropped. He wouldn't hit her. Not when he wanted something.

'C'mon Debbie,' he coaxed, 'it'll be OK.'

'Like hell it will!' she flung back. 'Just like last time? Who got caught? Who got the fines?' Where were you then?' She sneered. 'No where! Off your face somewhere else. as usual! As bloody usual!'

She circled around him. Punching his arm as she emphasised each word.

'You bastard! Not this time! Get it out! Everything! Out! You get out too!' Debbie's rejection of him as well was a surprise and he backed down. 'I mean it,' she said steel voiced. 'Get out of my house.'

Tony roughly elbowed past her.

The child in the kitchen howled with rage as his saucepan lids were kicked away. They skidded and rattled across the floor.

The back door banged. Hard.

Debbie's breathing was tight in her chest. Why had she put up with him? He had done nothing for her or the kids. Now this again. Drugs. She knew she had her faults but she'd not used drugs. Not since she had the kids anyway.

Her hands unclenched and she began to rip the foil down from the walls. Long wide strips fell in silver curtains. As she tore the window's covering free the light returned and the silver was a frothing whispering sea about her feet.

In the driveway Tony slumped into the front seat of his ute. He fisted the steering wheel in frustration.

Frustration at Debbie. At himself. He swore out loud. Didn't she know he could make heaps of money for them? As usual he could not argue with her. Not without striking her. Punching her again. He pulled a face ruefully as he thought of her standing up to him. She was quite a bird. It was a good thing she was seeing she had to look after the kids on her own. The last one was his and, in a way, he was proud of it. He lit a cigarette and pulled the smoke hard down into his lungs.

Still – his anger returned; he had a problem. Or his sponsor did. The one putting up the money. The one who would get most of the profits.

He punched the wheel again and pulled his mobile phone from his pocket. Dialled and waited. The connection was made.

'I told you the bitch wouldn't go for it!'

He started the engine, revved it loudly. Listened to the response. Grunted, then disconnected the phone. Flicking his cigarette butt out the window and he backed out of the driveway.

As he turned Tony could see the figure of the elderly neighbour as she appeared at her door. Tony jerked a rude finger gesture at her and roared away down the street.

Mrs. Harris smiled smugly. She could give tit for tat, and she kept notes. Wrote it all down. The woman was all right. The children were good too. Debbie tried. Even pulled out the weeds in the garden. Mrs Harris looked toward the yard where a red bottlebrush was flowering. Birds, honey eaters, swarmed and argued in the branches. That noise she could put up with. But him?

His music? His language and the fights when he was home? No! Debbie began to gather together the aluminium foil. She scrunched it, quickly made a large silver ball of it.

She pressed the foil ball hard. Sculpted it with anger. This was the last time. Tony was out of her life. As of now! She'd shove his gear into black garbage bags. Leave them out in the yard. With the drug stuff. Serve him right if someone pinched the lot.

She rubbed her hand tiredly down her face.

Enough was enough!

A laugh suddenly bubbled up. It gurgled past her lips and burst out into the air around her. Air and space that rarely heard her laugh. She whirled around arms flung wide. Danced to her own inner music. Free!

She didn't need him. Not him or anyone like him!

She would make changes... On her own.

Her thoughts surfaced in bursts as the laughter had. One after another. There was a course at TAFE she could do. Make use of the good marks she had got at school. 'Could have got into uni,' she reflected. Deferred then because of her first pregnancy in those wild teenage years. 'That no-hoper was long gone,' she thought. 'Now Tony...' She pushed the errant thoughts back and the feelings of optimism returned.

The toddler wobbled uneven steps to her from the kitchen. Grabbed at her legs in a steadying hug. She scooped him up. Wiped his dirty nose on a tissue she thrust back into her bra and planted a loud raspberry kiss into his neck. She put him down on the floor and rolled the silver foil ball to the beaming child.

'Here kiddo... You have this.' She laughed. Bitterness gone. 'We'll be better off on our own.'

She triumphantly crossed to the table, uncapped a beer and took a swallow.

SMILE AND SMILE...

'Watch out for this one...' I thought as I sat on the bus. I'd seen him as the bus passed a block back and now, he had managed to run hard enough to catch it. Somehow in that instant of seeing him we'd locked eyes and now he sat opposite me in the backward facing seat. He was puffing hard.

I was inwardly amazed at the physical presence of the man. He was, to put it bluntly, stunningly handsome. Tall, six-foot, late 30's with perfect teeth and hair, a strong muscular physique from probably many hours in gyms, blue eyed and smiling face.

He grinned across the miniscule space between us, all white teeth and sparkling eyes. But something about that smile did not compute. The eyes; the smile sparkled but it didn't crinkle the eyes. Somewhere I'd read 'to beware smiles where the eyes didn't crinkle'. The smile wasn't real. There was something about his posture too...a hidden threat?

He leaned forward, 'Crikey, I just about missed the bus,' he said. There was that smile again, missing the eyes. His hand almost touched my knee and I pulled back slightly. I was probably super aware because of the newspaper and TV accounts and warnings about a young rapist, who attacked and murdered, older women, often in their own homes. I'm an older woman, and with the rest of society's older women, I was on guard.

My response was just to half smile and nod. My body language closed up and I looked away and out the window.

Why, I wondered, did a man have to do that to women, when many women would have been his more than willing partners.

My journey was towards my home and it was just coming on

to evening and the darkness beginning. Instinct told me to continue to the shopping centre and police station further down the bus route. Hang overstaying on my pensioners' ticket. Covertly, I watched him in the reflection of the glass window.

'Going far?' he suddenly asked.

I started. 'Only to the shopping centre,' I said and then, realizing that I'd told him where I was going, I added, 'And to the police station. I lost my purse...' I lied lamely.

'Yeah,' he said.

After passing my own stop I got off the bus at the shopping centre. He did too and walked fifty metres behind me. I quickly went into the police station and paused at the door, not sure if he was still following. I could not see him but hurried inside. Now I was faced with appearing to be one of those panicking older woman, which I suppose I was.

As I fronted up to the young policeman behind the desk, the man, who was following me. came in.

'Hi Jack,' the desk man said. 'Been on bus duty?'

'Yeah,' Jack replied. 'This lady's lost her purse...'

He went into the back section after an amused nod to me. He knew I lied. But something told me that he was not quite the man they thought he was. Realizing my perhaps paranoia, maybe it's the paranoia of age, or maybe of life, an image of a cat amongst pigeons or of Shakespeare's words – 'to smile and smile and be a villain' hovered in my head.

I left quickly, after making my excuses, and caught a taxi home.

It is now about ten o'clock and I can see that the streetlight outside my home is broken, and the front of the house is quite dark.' Kids again with their stones,' I thought. The doorbell rang softly and I could see the shape of a tall person standing on my doormat. It rang again, still softly. I answered it.

'Your purse was handed into the station,' the man who was a

policeman said. He held out a purse that wasn't mine. 'You'll have to sign for it.' His foot held the door open and he smiled. The smile did not crinkle his eyes, yet again. 'May I come in?' he continued, as the door shut behind him…

THE NECKLACE AND THE SEA

In the morning, the sea was rough, very rough, and waves broke over the boat's bow and smashing into the cockpit area. it sent freezing water swirling around at thigh level, before it flooded out through the gunnels and away. Last night's incident, about the beads, came back into my mind as I battled my sea sickness demons. The owner's wife came on deck. She had taken a carved camel bone bead necklace from the secure cabinet below and now it hung around her neck.

'Why have you got that on?' I screamed above the sounds of the storm.

She silenced me with a stare that sent shivers, more than the cold waters down my neck.

She faced into the wind.

How does one describe her stance on the deck? She raised her hands and despite the fact that we all needed two hands to brace ourselves and to hang on for dear life, she stood there, solid as a rock, beside the mast. The beads hung rigid from her neck and with one hand she gathered them and held them out to the storm like an offering. Her other palm was flattened down against the seas. The beads took a shaft of light and as she swept her hand sideways the waters followed and calmed before the boat. All around the seas raged and we sailed into a puddle of still water.

'How did you do that?' I yelled.

She stared through me and snapped her hand shut. The calm waters vanished and the sea threw the boat sideways, almost capsizing us, before she opened her hand again and the sea subsided.

The necklace continued to glow.

She stood there for another hour like a figure head, until the storm had passed. Then she slumped, grabbing the mast and staggered down below to lock the necklace back into its cabinet. When she turned to us it was as if nothing had happened and she smilingly asked only if she could get everyone hot tea.

It was then we realised that she knew nothing of what had just happened.

I looked towards the cabinet and the beads hung slack, moving with the motion of the boat. They no longer glowed.

EDDY

For one instant he had the prize. He surfaced and held it high; felt the heady rush, heard the cheering then the pain exploded. He clasped the prize to his chest and sank below the choppy blue waters.

Pushing his glasses further up his nose, the Coroner looked around the institutional cream of the small country Court. He nodded towards the pathologist standing behind a paper strewn table. 'So, your basic report is that Edward Hanchant suffered a massive coronary occlusion and not that he drowned?'

'Yes, sir, it is.'

'Anything more to add?' he asked reflecting that this inquiry was probably another drab and sterile reflection of a man's life and death.

'Only that he led a hard life with extensive wear and tear on his body and joints. The body had numerous old scars. Surgical and injury scars. I can't remember seeing one like it.'

Instinctively the Coroner's gaze went towards the only intimate indication of the deceased Edward Hanchant; the black and white photograph of a nondescript man that lay on his grey desk.

'Thank you. You may step down.'

He glanced towards the police officer waiting his turn. 'OK, Bob, you're next.'

The country policeman flicked his papers and began. 'Edward Hanchant has proved to be an enigma,' he said. There was a shuffle in the room as interest was quickened from the formal to the potentially interesting. 'I can find no record of him anywhere and that photograph is the only one we have. He didn't like his photo being taken. No Centrelink contact although he reportedly told his friends he was on a pension; no Medicare number and he's got no police record of any type and never had an Australian driver's licence.'

'So, you think he may have reinvented himself? Not unusual to find single men like this in remote country areas. Getting away from relationships, marriages or simply disappearing.'

'Yes, I know he did.' Bob Richards paused for an instant for a little dramatic effect. 'We sent his dabs, his DNA, for comparison with records. The results are in.' The policeman gestured towards the photograph. 'Eddy is actually Raymond Fitzgerald. He was originally in the Australian Army but after an honourable discharge he disappeared and the next ASIO heard of him of was as a mercenary. A soldier for hire. The records of him are few but ASIO had him fighting, mainly in Africa, for whatever skirmish was paying the most money for soldiers.'

There seemed to be an intake of collected breaths and the Coroner glanced towards the back of the room where a teenager waited on a bench. 'I'll call you back, Bob, after we've heard from young Richard. He needs to get back to school.'

As he was sworn in Ricky Page looked less than eager to hurry his appearance in the court.

'Just tell your story Richard. Start with how long you've known the deceased.'

'Since I was a kid,' the sun-bleached teenager said. The lad being just fifteen brought a 'go on' smile from the bench. 'I'd see Eddy around and he always said 'hello'. He'd say that he'd get the Cross next year when we dived for it...'

'You mean at the Blessing of the Fleet. So, Eddy was a religious man?'

Ricky scratched at a mosquito bite on a sunburned arm. 'No. Never saw him in church, just that he'd dive for the Cross each year. He couldn't get down to the bottom, so he'd never got near it.'

'But you did, most years?'

'Yes Sir,' Ricky remembered his instructions and added the Sir. 'But Eddy'd try and try again even though we all laughed at the old codger trying to dive down that far. It's more than ten metres deep where they toss it in. After I'd got the Cross and given it up to the priest he'd be hanging onto the jetty and gasping like a fish out of water.'

'So, what happened this year?'

'I got the Cross off the bottom, as usual beating everyone else to it,' a smug smile creased his freckled face, 'suddenly I felt sorry for the old bloke and passed it to him as I swam up to the surface.' The Coroner nodded another 'go on'. 'He looked surprised but he took it. Then I came up and Eddy followed.'

'Did he look in distress?'

'Not then. He held the Cross up and got the Blessing. A bit later he just sank. We dived for him. I grabbed him by his hair, and brought him to the steps. Doc Williams was there and he did some resuscitation and they got the ambulance. Next thing we heard was that he was dead.'

'Did you like Eddy?'

'Yes Sir. We all did. We'd see him fishing from the jetty. He'd talk to us; ask us about school and sport. He barracked for one of the poncy AFL teams while we all went for rugby.'

'Was there anything else unusual about him that you saw?'

'No Sir, but he did always talk proper. It didn't go with his face or his tatty dog.'

'Thank you, Ricky. You have been very helpful. You can go now.' The Coroner noted a hesitation. 'Was there anything else?'

'Yes. I didn't kill him, did I? Giving him the Cross?'

'No Ricky. But I'm sure that your priest has told you that.'

'Yes Sir. But I wanted to hear it from you and the copper...'

Bob Richards took the stand again.

'Raymond Fitzgerald's pension,' the police officer put the word pension in gestured parenthesis, 'came from an overseas source we're still trying to trace. It's not from Britain and it's probably one of the tax or bank havens. It exactly matches the Australian pension and arrives on pension day. Very clever.'

'Have you discovered anything from his residence?'

'He owned the shack he lived in on the beach. It's not worth much and we can find no next of kin. We searched it and found a couple of things. A packet of medals was taped at the back of a drawer; that's what got us contacting the military. There was only one significant document. A will.'

'A will?' the coroner echoed. 'That I didn't expect. In the name of Edward Hanchant?'

'Yes Sir. It's been assessed at the law firm in the next town, they drew it up and they say that it's perfectly legal. That's even given now that we know he was Raymond Fitzgerald.'

'Has the law or anyone else got any claim on the money?'

'No Sir. None that we can find.'

'So, who are the beneficiaries of his will?'

'Mrs Tyler of the café. She made his evening meal each day. She gets his shack and everything there. But his pension, that's the interesting one.' Again, his hand made the air brackets.

'O! Who gets that? The Coroner asked.

'Part of it goes to the local RSPCA – providing they take his dog.' The policeman paused maybe for dramatic effect. 'The other part goes to UNICEF to sponsor children in Africa.'

'Given what you've said about him being a mercenary in Africa that seems reasonable.'

'But Sir, according to his Will the money is to be sent fortnightly to both groups, like he was sending his pension, until all the money is gone.'

'And was there any indication when that might be?' the

Coroner asked.

'No sir...that's the interesting part.'

The coroner made some final notes.

'An interesting case,' he mused. 'Here we have a man with two identities. One was an ex-mercenary who chose to become a nonentity. We have a boy who chose to help an old man realise his perhaps repentance Blessing, and a gift to a woman who nurtured him and another that will come to institutions one pension style cheque at a time. Could be substantial or only a few dollars left...' He looked around the quiet court. 'My judgement is that Raymond Fitzgerald also known as Edward Hanchant, aged probably sixty five years of age, died of natural causes in the act of over-excursion. Case closed.'

He gathered up his papers and grinned at the police officer who approached the bench.

'Anything else?'

'Just got a text, Sir. From ASIO. The bank source is Switzerland and it's a numbered account. As you would know, recently they had to divulge information on these accounts and when ASIO asked them they thought that this money may have been fraudulently banked.'

'It wasn't?'

'No. Not as it turned out. Being a mercenary isn't against the law unless the persons are fighting as a traitor.'

'So, the money?'

'It's millions, Sir.'

The coroner smiled. 'Well, perhaps Edward Hanchant got his redemption in getting the Cross, and giving his money away.'

'Redemption can take a while in this case, Sir.'

'Yes, Bob,' the coroner raised his eyebrows. 'A while...?'

Yes Sir, in maybe a couple of hundred years.'

THE JOURNEY

Jessica got into the car and slammed the door shut.

'A good start to a long trip.' her mother, Beth, thought with some irony. Neither of them wanted this journey but there was no option. 'C'mon, let's go.' she said aloud, her manner determined and cheerful, 'The sooner we clear the city the better. Before the morning rush gets too heavy.'

An hour later they were well on their way with green vineyards slipping by and the sun already ripening the grapes hanging in fat knobbly bunches. There were six hundred kilometres still before them to the distant uncle's funeral. Beth glanced sideways at her daughter. She was not impressed. Jessica, in her late 20's, was slumped in designer minimalist; jeans, a sweatshirt and grungy track soiled runners. Her shining red hair was a mess of pseudo tangles. Beth resigned herself, 'That's how they wear it these days...' she thought, 'looking like they've just got out of bed.' An olfactory clue nagged her memory.

'What's the perfume you're wearing Jess?' she asked, as much to break the silence as to find out.

'It's a spicy thing I got as a sample,' Jessica replied, opening one eye, 'Can't remember the name. It's different though, isn't it? I quite like it.'

Memory jolted. Of course! Great Aunt Dorothea. Beth remembered her and a similar scent from her childhood.

The images formed. Dorothea was old – even then, but tall and angular in body...yes... and she had that same smoky husky voice. Her hair formed a dark cap about her head and she wore elegant silk shirts, black trousers and smelt of spicy perfumes. She punctuated conversations with an ebony cigarette holder and clouds of pungent smoke. Though an early feminist and independent woman, already in the late 1940s, yet paradoxically Beth's mother helped her with her housework.

They had visited Aunt Dorothea weekly, travelling two noisy stops on the tram to her small rented flat next to an antique shop. Her own mother wouldn't talk about the family enigma but Beth gleaned fragments in snippets from the multitude of pictures and mementos heaped in Aunt Dorothea's treasure-trove flat. She was regularly allowed to have the exotic postage stamps from airmail envelopes strewn about or tucked into books, as markers. Sometimes she delved into Aunt Dorothea's wardrobe, where richly extravagant clothing hung in textures and colours that Beth had never seen in those post-war days. Dressing up games were a regular and exciting treat.

While her mother 'did' for her seven-year-old Beth questioned everything. She turned out drawers and presented things she found for explanation to her great aunt.

Stroking a photograph made sepia by time and handling, Aunt Dorothea would respond, 'This one was taken in London – at the Savoy. We'd meet Lord 'So-and-So' there for drinks after the theatre.' Or 'That was an art deco broach I'd worn on her hat to Royal Ascot.' Aunt Dorothea held her pictures and belongings to her throat and voyaged back and forth in a prematurely muddled mind. Beth adored her and the fantasy life she glimpsed.

'Mum, you're in a day-dream. Do you want me to drive for a while?' Jessica suddenly interrupted. They changed places at the next gas station, refuelling and buying bottled drinking water. Jessica relaxed as she took the wheel. She liked driving and this was a better car than the claptrap vehicle she owned. 'You were a long way away, Mum. You usually give me the third degree when we get together.' She paused. 'You didn't want to give up your painting time for this funeral either, did you?' Jessica loved baiting

Beth and as the car sang past the wheat stubble paddocks that had taken over from the grapes, her question was intended to mildly provoke.

'No. It's not that. We should attend this funeral. Uncle Peter was the last of my mother's brothers,' Beth answered smiling. 'Something, your perfume I think, reminded me of my great Aunt Dorothea. She's been gone for ages, but suddenly here she was again. It's been years since I thought of her.'.

'She's the one in that silver frame in the hall? The one Dad said I look like?'. Jessica questioned as her interest was piqued.

Beth looked at her daughter considering. 'You know he's right. There is a resemblance. Shall I tell you a bit about her? It'd pass the time.'

Jessica nodded. 'Yes please.'

'Well,' Beth started with the family pedigree – that would place her. 'Aunt Dorothea was my maiden great aunt, on my mother's side. As a young woman she was an exceptional beauty, intelligent and witty. Her class-conscious parents had great aspirations for her. No local suitors thank you! She was to marry well and they were determined to bask in her reflected wealth and glory. So, suitably chaperoned, she was sent to Europe on a finishing 'Grand Tour' to find an acceptable husband, a baronet at least.'

Jessica snorted, 'Did they still do those sorts of things when you were young?'

'Of course not – that was years before I was born.' Beth glanced sideways and laughed. 'Anyway, when her chaperone was hit by a horse and carriage and she died in Rome, Aunt Dorothea took her chance to escape the genteel and boring itinerary. Her parents contacted the British Embassy and they instructed her to return to Australia.'

'I said 'No!' she'd dramatically say to me when she remembered, 'I will stay in Europe.' On her parents' insistence, the Embassy sent someone to escort her to the docks and a ship back to Australia but she slipped away from them. 'She had a marvellous sense of theatre and like an actress, Aunt Dorothea would re-enact her flight by train and boat across Europe to London, for me, again and again. It was very exciting. In those days, a young woman excelling in horsemanship was encouraged in the 'best society' – it showed spirit in them as well as in men – and before she left Australia Dorothea had shown exceptional ability. She'd made equestrian contacts in England, and this was her entrance to be invited and to stay at many grand houses in 1930s. Her parents had no option and reluctantly allowed her to remain there. It also put her where they wanted her; amongst the wealthy families with titles...'

Beth laughed at the wry outcome.

'But she was unchaperoned, and she probably had a bit too much freedom and fun in the London nightclubs. Before long, her name and pictures were published in the London newspapers. Australian papers inevitably picked up the spicy society stories,' her mother continued.

'What – paparazzi already in those days?' Jessica was incredulous.

'Yes, nothing's new. The tabloid reports caused great consternation to her parents and stern telegrams were sent demanding she come home immediately. They through that if she were suitably repentant, she could still fulfil their amended ambitions in the local marriage market,' Beth laughed.

'But she ignored them and stayed away – wouldn't you have too? Outraged, they promptly cut off her allowance and, in their indignation, they never spoke her name again.' 'Never? 'Jessica said dryly. 'So, I'm not the first person in the family to disappoint her parents.' Her mother started to protest but Jessica grunted a chuckle and Beth instead continued the saga.

'One day I found some tiny baby clothing in a satin pillow case tucked away in a drawer.' Beth hesitated and glanced sideways again at her daughter. Jessica's eyes didn't falter from the road ahead and Beth went on. 'I asked Aunt Dorothea about them.'

'O my dear, my dear…' she had said in tearful drama.

'Those represented the great love of her life – a forbidden relationship with an influential titled person. She bore twin sons to him but the premature babies died at birth. There was great scandal. My mother whisked the box away from me and that subject was closed.'

'That must have been awful,' Jessica commented flatly. 'What happened to her after that?'

'Well – Aunt Dorothea stayed with the man and the couple partied on the fashionable world stage for quite a while,' Beth said with a smile at her daughter, '…and they continued to make the Australian newspapers.' Her tone changed as her memory shifted. 'They went their different ways when the Second World War broke out. Even then Aunt Dorothea's life was a mystery. Some boxes I found held pieces of military insignia and bundles of photographs. Many showed her dressed stylishly in elegant clothing and in others she wore military uniform and sat at the wheel of army staff cars. She accompanied high-ranking men in London, to Paris after the liberation and to the bomb devastated city of Berlin…

'There were hints of duty, secrets and of things best left unsaid. That's the impression I remember. My mother would often try to shut her aunt up at that point.' Beth chuckled at the memory. 'Beth doesn't need all the details' she'd say. Anyway, Aunt Dorothea continued her globe-trotting life for a few years after the war then abruptly she came home.'

'It all sounds, to me, as if she was a high-class whore in uniform. Maybe a spy.' Jessica stated dryly. She pulled into the agreed lunch stop. They sat still in the car caught up in the drama and the remembering. 'Come on Mother, don't stop now.'

'Later,' Beth paused looking at her daughter, said. 'Jess, I do wish you'd dressed a bit nicer. I hope you have better clothing for the funeral?'

'Mother, I'm alright in these clothes today.' Jessica's voice dropped in exasperation. 'Why must you always remind me about things? I do know what's required. For Pete's sake cut me some slack!' Jessica got out of the car and marched into the little bakery shop.

'I've done it again,' Beth remonstrated herself. 'Got her slamming doors.'

The barriers were up again. Lunch was bought and eaten with a studied politeness between them in the car. Beth was very aware of the atmosphere as she was of the differences in their attitudes reflected in their dress. Jessica was university educated but she had not, in her mother's opinion, lived up to her ability and opportunity. Beth, in contrast, was self-taught and financially, a successful artist. She dressed the part in an elegant self-portrait.

After lunch Beth took over the driving and without consultation continued the saga.

'Occasionally,' she started, 'Aunt Dorothea would stay over-night with us. I'd give up my bed for her and she kept me awake with her snoring!' She laughed. 'But when I was about ten years old things changed. Aunt Dorothea was no longer fascinating; instead, she sat dreaming and muttering to herself. The weekly trips had become a bore and I'm afraid I visited reluctantly. She seemed to exist on cigarettes and brandy she'd become a worry.'

'Mother and Dad talked about finding a nursing home, an acceptable alternative in those days. Then one day – Aunt Dorothea just died. When the neighbours in the shop hadn't not seen her for a day or so they called the police and Mother was contacted as her next of kin.'

'You mean that was it, she died?' Jessica demanded. 'All that preamble and that was it? Really Mother...was it suicide?'

Beth was serious. 'You've got to understand I was pretty young and suicide was never mentioned; certainly not in my hearing. But in hindsight it was probably brandy mixed with sleeping tablets. Her will instructed that she was to be cremated immediately, without ceremony. That wasn't usual and caused many whispered conversations. Anyway, after the funeral my mother and I went to clear up her flat for the last time. I was very excited and I couldn't wait to get my greedy hands into all the thrilling stuff that waited to be sorted out.'

'But Aunt Dorothea's flat was virtually empty. Just a few forlorn bits of furniture and little pieces of jewellery she'd left to Mother were waiting for us. That was all! Her last actions had been to completely erase herself. Everything exotic and everything I wanted was gone – sold or burnt in the backyard incinerator. Mother was not surprised, and I believe, she was somewhat relieved. Me!' Beth laughed at the memory, 'I was totally put out! '

'Definitely a whore.' Jessica interrupted, 'And some of this family stuff has been repeated?'

'What on earth do you mean?' Beth was startled.

'Mother, you've been organising me for years. Just like Aunt Dorothea's parents did. 'Go to uni.' OK that was good, but the eternal – 'do something with your talents'. The pressure – it never ends!' She paused. '...I've always let you down.'

Beth opened her mouth to deny her daughter's accusations. She hesitated, then was silent for a long moment.

'Has this been the way you have thought about us, mother and daughter?' she finally asked quietly.

'I know you love me, Mum. I'm not sure they loved Dorothea, not from what you've said.'

Jessica chuckled, despite her outburst. 'Mother – I'm not going to squander my abilities or my education. I'm ambitious and I'm working on some great projects. I just don't want to talk about them yet. I will in time – when I'm ready.'.

Beth pulled the car over onto the verge and stopped the engine. 'Jess,' she began carefully. 'We never talked much about your trip to Europe, about the baby and...' her voice hesitated. 'There always seemed to be barriers between us.' She noted the glistening tears appearing in Jessica's eyes. 'I know I wasn't the mother you needed then. Too much tied up in my own work probably, but... you rejected us so totally. I couldn't reach you...not then, and even now I...'

Jessica wiped her fingers across her eyes, suddenly the wild determined child again, but this time without the defiant head toss away that usually covered her emotions.

'Mum, you can't blame yourself! When I was in Europe with Pierre it was the most wonderful and the most terrible time of my life. I couldn't share it... and when little Amy came and Pierre went away, I was too shattered and too angry; too proud too, to talk to anyone.'

Jessica stopped and looked into her mother's now tearful face. 'I was wrong too. Mother, you and Dad probably loved me too much. You encouraged me too much. So much...that I couldn't admit that Pierre had been anything other than a tragic mistake. Never baby Amy though...' Her voice faltered.

Beth sat with her arms about her daughter until slowly both were composed again. 'I didn't really see the parallels between you and Aunt Dorothea until now,' she mused quietly, then she leaned over the back seat to gaze at the sleeping baby, Amy, safe in her carry cot. She unclipped a small ivory edelweiss broach from her blouse and placed it in her daughter's hands.

'Maybe this should be yours,' she said. 'It was Aunt Dorothea's and I don't know why I wore it today. Maybe I was meant to and all this was necessary between us.' She laid her hand on her daughter's cheek; the bond warm and loving then she restarted the car to continue their journey.

BY WHATEVER MEANS...

'Now, let me get this right, Mr. Rexel, you're trying to tell me that you're not Tony Rexel.' She paused. 'You deny being Rexel? You say you're someone else?'

The young detective looked amused. She was a good–looking bird. Serious like, but OK, with dark hair drawn back into a loose bun thing. A sort of Irish complexion – all peaches and cream. Her figure matched the face. I could get to like someone like that, I thought. I've always gone for the Irish look.

'Right,' she scoffed. 'And that would explain the fingerprints we have on file matching yours?'

I managed to hide my reaction. My fingerprints matched this Rexel's? Must be a mistake.

'Never heard of this Rexel person,' I repeated my mantra blandly.

She tapped the photograph comparing my face with the photograph she held. 'His mug shot faxed in from interstate looks remarkably like you. We know about you, Rexel.' She'd dropped the amused look with the 'mister'. 'White collar crime, forgery and passing bum cheques, big ones,' she said sternly. 'It might be the first time you've operated here – but who do you think you're kidding?'

I gave her the raised eyebrows look and said nothing.

'Interview halted at 2.57 pm.,' she said abruptly into the tape recorder.

She picked up files, photographs, fingerprint sheets and the cups from the table and walked out. A tactic used in police examinations I guessed from movies I'd seen over the years. I was left alone in the cold bare room. Idly I wondered if a mirror on the wall was two-way. Sure, and probably there was a video camera there too. I smoothed my hair back. I'd be cool and calm. Being brought in for questioning. This interview, and the Rexel character, I hadn't expected any of it.

Two months ago, I'd had an intriguing proposition put to me and a new life beckoned. It went with an astonishing offer of $100,000 – to be transformed. Surgically transformed. I thought. It must be a scam and, looking back now in hindsight, maybe it's true. It looked like this Rexel character was maybe the key to my current predicament.

I leaned back on the hard steel chair, relaxed for the camera, and let my mind go back. It all seemed up front.

There I was sitting in the library and this doctor approached me and offered me new ears. Now this may seem funny to you but if you've lived with ears that resemble huge, white fat butterflies all your life, having someone offer you new ones is a proposition you listen to. It was an experimental procedure, he said. A new one, untried in this country. That's why there was this money to go with it, in case of problems. Who would ask questions? Not me! With ears that stood out like 747 wings – I was all for it!

That afternoon I stood in the foyer of a discrete clinic, one that the celebs go to for their 'non-existent' plastic surgery. They operated on my ears, cut away acres of flesh, and they gave me a facelift too. A bonus! A few wrinkles less and I looked years younger. The skin taken from my fingers, they said, was to go on the reconstruction of my ears. It seemed OK to me. Holiday time with cute nurses, a real menu with good food and free grog. Hardly a hospital – more like a fancy hotel! Yes Mr Daniels, no Mr Daniels, would you like another red wine Mr Daniels? I stayed in the clinic for two weeks all expenses paid and the hundred grand waiting. Came out a new man. One checkup in six weeks then I'm off.

The transformation will be quite a change from my old life.

Before everything was dominated by ears that Prince Charles could have smiled smugly to himself about. His ears were moths besides my stinking butterflies! I was bullied at school and at home, always about the ears. I learned to hate people! I'd chucked my uni science course because of incessant taunts from other stupid students. Lecturers too! But by the time I'd left I'd learned enough to know where to go to look for the information I needed.

After uni, I'd decided on a new career.

Now, this Rexel deal has come as some surprise.

I looked around. First time in a police cell wasn't all that bad. I just had to keep the pretence up a bit longer. Be this Rexel character. So, he had a money-making racket and maybe I'd have to do a few years in prison before I could be off overseas with the nicely stashed away bundle.

Now I smiled. Maybe Tony Rexel had my face. My ears! Maybe I'd been picked for my height and build for a switch of identities.

Pity him if he looked like the old me now. I almost laughed out loud.

These same police could be getting too close to the old me. After they linked all the deaths, all the bodies, they were looking for a suspect, or so the papers said. Papers I'd read in the clinic. A guy with 'butterfly ears', it said. Dangerous, a psychopath, they'd shoot to kill. That wasn't fair, I felt, I didn't use violence. Or did I?

But my body count was impressive.

The doctor with the transformation offer should have checked the books I was reading in the library. He'd given me enough time to go home and pack a bag. Pack and leave the family for good, enjoying a meal. Their final meal. One I'd cooked while they lorded over me one last time. The usual jibes about the ears and 'no hopers.' I'd planned to try the new poison I was researching on them. If I'd learned anything from science it was that experimentation must evolve. A laugh, this new poison was better than the poison I'd been slipping into the fancy upmarket 'coffee and cake brigade' cups while working as their smiling, popular, looks good in tight pants, waiter.

Just a random drop into their cappuccinos, their lattes, their flat whites. Random's more revengeful. More satisfying.

Then they had gone off to die in their expensive homes.

I got quite good at it and I was only suspected after someone saw me without the wig I wore to cover my red hair and my ears. Someone got curious. The papers also said that the trail of the 'Butterfly Poisoner' had gone cold. He could have left town.

Transformation, yeah, I'd liked that! I knew I looked good now, handsome even. I had a laugh against Mr. Rexel now that I knew that he was a forger, a white-collar crim. Instinctively I'd insisted on cash. No cheques.

Doing time for Rexel, a pushover with my new looks, would distance me from the 'Butterfly Poisoner'.

It was all too easy...

I'd got what I wanted, and I'll do what I want...by whatever means...

Amy Haldane carefully donned gloves and placed the cup into a DNA evidence bag for forensics. This was the biggest 'sting' that the police department had ever witnessed. One given to them on a plate. They just had to follow it through. It was definitely illegal but there simply was no evidence linking the suspect, the anonymous man sitting in the interview room, to the dozens of poisoning victims that had occurred over the past years. They knew it was him but he'd been clever enough to avoid leaving DNA traces to link himself to the crimes.

Except once!

The transformation, the surgery, would get him for Rexel's crimes. The multi-millionaire criminal Rexel, who'd conveniently fronted up with inoperable cancer, near death offering himself. Maybe it was a redemption? His scheme to trap a killer, his millions offered without explanation.

They'd surgically lifted his prints for this operation and remodelled the man they wanted. Once they had him, the pseudo-Rexel in prison, they could get legitimate legal DNA to get him for the murders. They'd got a DNA sample from the carnage of his home before he went into the clinic. A carnage they hadn't expected. Testing the cup was illegal, as the suspect, under current law could not be tested without his consent. Consent no criminal ever gave without conviction. Once he was in prison they had him. He'd be tested there without his permission.

Convict him for life on the evidence – throw away the key!

Senior Detective Amy Haldane took a deep breath. She straightened her hair, practiced a small smile, and went back to continue the charade against the man who had randomly slipped the extra something into peoples' cappuccinos, into unknown peoples' coffee.

Maybe into Rexel's mother's latte? He hated her for her for her indifference to his ears, his butterfly ears. The ears she gave him at birth. They'd never know, Rexel died without telling them anything.

Into Amy's own mother's coffee! The pain was still deep. Never ending.

Detective Haldane thought, 'By whatever means...'

www.ingramcontent.com/pod-product-compliance
Lightning Source LLC
Chambersburg PA
CBHW070024120726
47909CB00003B/1047